Also by Shontaiye

All 4 Da Doe 2
Deceit, Lies, and Alibi's
Deceit, Lies, and Alibi's 2

Coming Soon by Shontaiye

Blood 4 My Brother
Wrong Turn
Thru the Eyes of a Hoodrat
Thru the Eyes of a Jackboy

◇◇◇

Contact us:
uptownbookspublications.com
uptownbookspublication@yahoo.com
uptownshontaiye@yahoo.com

All 4 Da Doe

SHONTAIYE

Uptown Books
1147 S. Salisbury Blvd
Suite 8-191
Salisbury, MD, 21801

This is a work of fiction. All of the characters, organizations, and events portrayed in this novel are either products of the author's imagination or are used fictitiously.

All 4 Da Doe. Copyright © 2014 Uptown Books. All rights reserved. No part of this book may be used or reproduced in any manner whatsoever without written permission except in the case of brief quotations embodied in critical articles or reviews.

ISBN-13: 978-0-9863212-0-7
ISBN-10: 0986321206

ACKNOWLEDGEMENTS

I would like to thank anyone that has actually read my book. I appreciate being given an opportunity as a new writer. I thank my mama for giving me feedback and reading through a lot of my crap before the final product is done.

ONE

NEVER IN A million years would I had ever thought I would be the target of blackmail. Yet, here I was sitting by the phone shaking like a leaf. To say I was scared would be an understatement. My mama had always told me greed catches up with you, and it had surely caught up with my black ass.

I shifted around nervously while I waited for the caller to call back. The plush leather couch I sat on felt sticky against my sweaty skin. I tapped my foot nervously against the floor. I wasn't sure what my next move would be, but for now, the only option I had was to comply with the callers demands.

The phone rang harshly, causing me to jump. I took a deep breath, and swiped the answer button on my iPhone. The normally comfortable air-conditioned room, felt hotter than normal. Small beads of sweat had formed on my nose, but I didn't bother to wipe them off; I was focused on the message of the anonymous caller.

"I want half a million," the deep voice abruptly stated to me on the other line. "I know what you do, I know what you've made, and I want half…" The voice paused. "I'll text you the account information. You have a week. No funny shit, or I'll expose you bitches to the IRS."

The absence of sound alerted me that the call had been disconnected, so I slowly placed the phone back down beside me. I fell to the carpeted floor as the feeling of stress and grief washed over me. Dread sat in the pit of my stomach, while thoughts of what I would do flooded my mind. I didn't have that type of money to hand over to anyone. Certainly I had made it many times over during the course of several years, however, I had been a reckless spender and recently called myself investing some of the dirty money I had made in multiple ventures.

I only had about two hundred thousand in cash, but I did own my house, and I also had a handful of rental properties throughout the city. However, many of the rental properties required repair work that constantly required capital to go out. I also had just started buying equipment for a nail bar I was opening. I had assets but not a ton of cold cash like the caller wanted. And there was no way on God's green earth I was parting with all my cash.

The scheme I was involved in was supposed to be over. I had done it for a couple of years just to put me where I needed to be. At the time I had a job, but I needed a lump sum of money to secure me and my daughter's future.

Who the hell could that be that would do something like this to me? I would figure it out sooner or later, but for now I had to deal with saving my growing empire from the dirty world of extortion.

SHONTAIYE

◇◇◇

Briana looked at me from across her kitchen table with a tear stained face. The puffy bags around her eyes indicated that she had probably been crying all day.

"What are we gonna do Nina?" she asked me. "I don't have $250,000." She rose up from the table and retrieved the bottle of wine off the granite counter, refilling her glass for the second time in five minutes.

I sighed deeply. My head had begun throbbing earlier as the stress of the events weighed heavily on my mind. I didn't have the answer.

Massaging my temples with my left hand, I responded in a low voice without looking at her, "I don't know Briana."

Finally making eye contact I said, "I'm gonna sleep on this shit and maybe we can come up with something tomorrow. We gotta do something tho. If we sit around and do nothing, we're fucked. Onney will lose her job, and we'll fuck around and owe the IRS

Four years ago when Layla was four, she became suddenly ill. What began as a suspected cold, grew worse, and was eventually diagnosed as a severe case of Pneumonia. She spent four weeks in the hospital and went from a chubby, forty pound four year old, to a thirty pound child who would barely eat. It was devastating for me since I wasn't able to do anything for her pain, or be there for her like I wanted to. Layla wanted her mommy around the clock, but mommy had to bring in some sort of income to make sure we still had a place to live.

My job was more than understanding, but I still didn't have enough paid time off to take an extended leave from work to be with Layla like I wanted. Rashid had just got out of jail and would sit with her half the day, however, he worked second shift and was on parole so he eventually had to go to work. I ended up cutting my hours to be there with her the remainder of the day when he left, as well as overnight.

In that short month my finances took a

"Playin with my cousins. My daddy took us to Coco's fun house and we got in the bouncy," she revealed excitedly.

Coco's was a well-known local business. It was essentially a giant play room for kids, with oversized inflatable bounce houses they could jump on. They had some that resembled castles, dragons, and even characters like Thomas the Train.

"Oh wow honey. Sounds like you're having a ball. I'm jealous. Well you keep having fun, and mommy will come pick you up tomorrow. Tell daddy to have you ready around 12 ok. Love you babe, mwah!" I said, making kissing sounds into the phone.

"Ok mommy. Love you too."

I hung up the phone with the intention of calling back later to let Rashid know that I would be picking Layla up at noon tomorrow. I thought about how much I loved my daughter. She was the reason behind my madness. The reason why I woke, breathed, and ultimately schemed.

silently except for the sound of my Gucci Sofia high heeled booties tapping against Briana's hard wood floors.

After safely climbing into the driver seat of my black Mustang GT, I grabbed my iPhone from my glove compartment and called my daughter's father Rashid. He answered after the sixth ring.

"Damn what the fuck took you so long to answer the phone? Let me talk to Layla please."

Irritation poured from my voice. I hadn't even bothered to say hello. I hated when Rashid acted like he didn't see the phone ringing, when he knew damn well he was probably right on it texting. He always had his phone.

"Hi to you too Nina. My phone was in the other room. Hold on, here she go."

After a bit of shuffling, I finally heard my daughters' syrupy voice along with all the background noise.

"Hi mommy," she greeted me cheerfully.

"Hey baby, whatchu doing?" I asked, automatically changing the tone of my voice.

millions. And we'd definitely do jail time. We can't risk it. We're gonna have to pay them off. *How* we'll do that is the question? I don't wanna fuck with the illegal tax shit since that's what's got us jammed up in the first place. This shit is crazy. Fuckin hatin ass motherfuckers. Whoever the fuck it is."

"Have you even told Onney yet?" she asked through glassy eyes, while shifting around in her chair.

I rolled my eyes since Briana already knew the answer to the question she was asking.

"Of course not," I finally responded impatiently. "She didn't want to get involved from the beginning, but we begged her. Now this shit happens. For now I'm gonna wait. She'll flip when she hears this shit. On top of that, I don't trust Onney no further that I can spit. I wanna figure out our next move, and then let her know what's up."

I pushed my long black hair behind my ears and exhaled again deeply. I was still a little fidgety from earlier. After pondering over that dreaded call, I finally decided to call it an early day and make my way back home. I left blow. Since I was cutting my hours to be at the hospital, my income plummeted. On top of that, my insurance wasn't covering the entire cost of Layla's hospitalization. Just that quickly I was thrust into debt, and struggling to make ends meet. Rashid helped as much as he could, but it still wasn't enough. Luckily tax season had just approached, enabling me to use my returns to catch up on most of my bills.

When tax time did finally come, an idea ended up hitting me. Every year I watched people who sat on their ass all year filing fake returns. These same folks wound up getting back several thousand dollars for absolutely nothing. The majority of the time the IRS never caught them, even though they filed the dummy returns every year. Why couldn't I do that, just on a different level? I even had the perfect type of person to file the dummy returns for; prisoners. My scheming mind had a plan that would put me right where I needed to be.

The typical inmate never filed tax returns since he or she was incarcerated. My plan was to file dozens of fake returns and rake in thousands off each one. The first year I filed twenty fake returns and ended up with around $50,000 cash from Uncle Sam. That's when I decided that it's go big or go home. The second year I filed 100 with the help of my sister. The third and fourth year, 200. The last two years, Briana and I were bringing in almost a quarter million dollars apiece.

We only targeted inmates who had life sentences and would never see daylight again. The way we obtained their information was by sending letters with fraudulent contact information which stated that we were an organization that helped inmates get new trials, and get their convictions overturned. We asked for prison id number, case details, and ultimately, personal information such as date of birth, and social security numbers. Ninety-nine percent of these inmates willingly gave this information, with hopes that one day they would be free.

My older sister Onney works at one of the state prisons in upstate Pennsylvania. Heavy-set but pretty, Onney had always been a bit of a tomboy so it was fitting for her to take a job as a correctional officer. As a Lieutenant she is able to access information on inmates in Pennsylvania who have life in prison. With her connections, we had a list of "lifers," male and female, in Pennsylvania as well as the surrounding states. For that information we gave her 10% of what we brought in every tax season. Onney usually walked away with about $50,000 while Briana and I took home around $250,000.

The money literally changed my life. I was able to put Layla in private school, purchase stocks and bonds, buy several properties, take trips all over the world, and surround myself with items I could only have dreamed of. It was a risky situation that we knew we couldn't continue forever. Even though I had burnt through a lot of money, I had wised up the past year and had been investing my money so I would have something to build on, and be secure in the future. Briana didn't have children and blew money like it was nothing. I'm sure she wasn't broke, but I bet that she didn't have much to show from four years of scheming.

Onney on the other hand, I wasn't so sure about. She lived three hours away so we rarely saw much of her. She had been hesitant to go along with the plan initially, trying as best she could to minimize her involvement. It was actually Briana's idea to bring her in on everything

Before Onney's involvement I had been obtaining prisoner information online through public court records. Onney and I had never really been close, so I knew if anything every happened she would probably turn on us at the speed of lightning. One thing about me is that I had honor, so if shit ever hit the fan, my lips were sealed. However, I couldn't speak for anyone but myself.

I didn't sleep well that night with thoughts of possible prison time running through my mind. I didn't want my daughter to end up in the foster care system like I did. I didn't have any family besides my sisters, so my daughter would basically have no one if I got drug down behind this tax fraud shit. She had her dad part-time, but he was unreliable since he was in and out of jail for drugs. I had to think long and hard about my next move, so I could get out of the shit's creek I had fell in.

TWO

BOOM! BOOM!

The sound of banging at my door woke me abruptly out of my sleep. "What the fuck?" I asked no one in particular.

Still slightly disoriented, I jumped out of my warm bed and stumbled down the carpeted, but still cold hallway to the door to see who it was. After peering through the peephole, I saw that it was a smiling Rashid and Layla.

"What the hell is wrong with you?" I asked, clearly annoyed, while opening the door. "Why would you bang on the door like that? You scared me."

I wiped a small piece of crust out of my eye, and let the two of them in. Layla immediately dropped her bag, gave me a hug and kiss, then proceeded to her room to play with her volcano pile of toys. At her age she was happily self-absorbed.

"It's two o clock and I just came by to check on you since Layla said you would be by to pick her up at 12, " Rashid stated, quickly peering around the house and then turning his gaze to me.

Rashid's intense stare burned a hole through me, causing me to feel a little uncomfortable. Once I realized I jumped out of the bed with nothing on but my bra and thong, I understood why he had a damn eye problem.

At five foot four, I was extremely thick. I wasn't the ideal video vixen with the big ass and unrealistic small waist; I instead, was built like a brick house, thick all over and very bottom heavy. I wasn't fat though. I was one of those types that people assumed came from a family of voluptuous women. Hands down, my body turned heads. I was a black man's dream come true with a pretty, chocolate face to match.

"Damn, I overslept. And stop looking at me like that. Let me go put on sumn real quick."

I rolled my eyes and walked off to the back of my house to put on some clothes. My round chocolate ass jiggled as I made my way, and of course Rashid came following right behind it.

"You ain't gotta change. You straight. We need to talk anyway," Rashid said flirtatiously, while walking behind me into my room.

"Talk about what?" I snapped, still a little sleepy and irritated from being woken up. "Aint shit for me and you to talk about unless it's about Layla."

Ever since Rashid and I had broken up six years ago, he always wanted to "talk." I had no desire to entertain him unless it was about our daughter. One minute he pretended he was cool, then the next minute he wanted a family with us. To hell with all that. I had no desire to be with Rashid on that level anymore. Throughout the three years we were together, he did nothing but lie and cheat. During the time we were together he became arrogant, like I was supposed to put up with his shit. *And had the nerve to be jealous.* It also didn't help that he formed a habit of being in and out of jail.

"Damn Nina. I changed. I'm threw with that cheating and jail shit. Layla could use her dad around the house, and you could use the help. We could make it work, just on some mature shit this time," Rashid suggested, sounding sincere.

I took a deep breath and finally responded arrogantly. "Rashid honey…I'm good. I handle my own shit and got my own money. I don't have time to go backwards."

"What you fuckin somebody or sumn?" he asked with attitude. He frowned his face up jealously.

"Naa, it's not that. I'm just focused, and I don't have time to deal with the negativity you bring. I'm focused on a whole notha chapter of my life. And besides I know my worth."

Rashid just peered at me for ten seconds and I guess let what I said register.

"Whatever yo. Well at least let me fuck you. Ya ass got fat as shit." He reached over and grabbed me by my waist, pulling me into him.

That finally did it for me. I pushed away from him.

"Rashid get the fuck out. Hit me up when you wanna talk to Layla or pick her up. And why don't you be a good father and get her a phone so you can contact her directly."

Rashid shot me a dirty look. "Oh it's like that?"

"Yeah. It is."

"Aight cool. Ima say bye to my daughter real quick tho."

Rashid walked out of the room to go say bye to Layla and about thirty seconds later, I heard the door close. Damn I was glad he left. Rashid was such a pain in the ass. I peeped out the window to make sure he had left and decided to get myself together so I could make an early dinner for Layla.

Two hours later I had finished making our Sunday dinner of: smothered chicken wings, mashed potatoes, and green beans with tomatoes. I definitely put it down on Soul-food Sundays before it was time to be back to work on Monday.

Despite my illegal activities, I still worked forty hours a week as a Claims Rep for Aetna to maintain some level of normalcy. I had come along ways from being the poor little black Nina who was in and out of foster homes. I had never knew my father and my mother had been killed in a home invasion when I was ten. Briana was nine and Onney was fourteen when our lives were turned upside down by the tragic event. The rumor was she was killed in a crack house that was known for having heavy weight dealers around. Whoever robbed the spot wasn't taking any chances and leaving witnesses.

Even though my mom was a crack-head, she had been a functioning addict. She worked at a hotel, and for the most part we remained clean and fed. For some reason my mother just found comfort from getting high. She had struggled with depression for as long as I could remember, and after my grandmother passed away, she kind of zoned out. I guess the lost, along with depression and being a single mother, took its toll on her. She stopped functioning and got swallowed up by the streets, eventually dying in them.

My mom had a sister, but she too, was preoccupied with getting high to come help raise her orphaned nieces. She wasn't even close to being a functioning addict. She was one of those bad teeth, prostitute drug addicts. Ultimately, we wound up being in and out of foster homes until we turned 18. Onney ended up being separated from us since it was easier to place younger children. No one really wanted to be bothered with foul-mouthed, emotional and problematic teenagers.

Luckily for me and Briana, we had a good caseworker who worked hard at keeping us together. We never stayed gone from one another long, since our worker Ms. Evans, always fought tooth and nail to get us both placed in the same home. However, we often times went months without speaking to Onney, who over time, turned into someone we barely knew. Even to this day she is very isolated and secretive. It took us months to learn she had moved to Northern Pennsylvania to take a job as a corrections officer. Even when she got married to another C.O, it was unknown to us and discovered months later through a general conversation.

After Layla went to bed I decided to relax and reflect back on yesterday's events. I poured a glass of my favorite red wine, and proceeded to run myself a hot bath in the oversized tub that drew me to buy the home in the first place.

I looked around my private master bath and realized how much I had. Clearly, I hadn't earned it *all*, but something inside of my mind forced me to believe that I was entitled to it all. I deserved the small, but beautiful townhome in the upscale development that I lived in. I deserved to be able to take trips to Aruba to lie on a beautiful beach with green water. Yes, *green* water, not blue.

I grew up in foster homes. I went to home after home where I wasn't wanted. When I turned eighteen I was on my own and essentially homeless, living in a shelter until I was able to get a job that allowed me to afford a small room. That same room I shared with Briana when she became of age, until we were finally able to get an apartment. I worked my ass off for years and finally got a break when I graduated from community college and got a job with Aetna. Didn't I deserve all that I had, no matter how I obtained it? Needless to say, no one could tell me otherwise.

THREE

It was the following Monday, so I dropped Layla off at her private school bright and early at 8:15. I had taken the day off so I could make my way around and verify repairs were being made on several of my properties. After speaking with my contractor and visually verifying repairs, I was pleased.

It was 2:15 when I sat down in the small booth at Chili's downtown. All four of my properties were in North Philly, so it was convenient to have lunch there. I checked the time on my rose gold Michael Kors watch; Briana was running late as usual, so I decided to order some spinach dip to quiet the hunger pangs in my stomach.

I had eaten all of my appetizer and was nibbling on dry nachos when Briana showed up. It was 3pm and the bitch was almost an hour late. Luckily for her, I was a laid back person and I didn't sweat the small shit.

"Wassup chick, what took you so long?" I asked, before taking a sip of water.

"Girl you know traffic in Philly is terrible. Plus I had to drop off my homeboy." She looked cute with a royal blue paint suit on and oversized gold accessories. A messy bun complimented her funky look.

"Homeboy? I aint heard about no homeboy--," I said, before pausing. I was extremely curious, but I remained quiet. Briana loved to talk, and showing interest but keeping quiet, was my way of silently encouraging her to spill. This way I could avoid asking, and appearing nosey.

"You don't remember Eric? We met him at the casino. Tall, dark-skinned, with the tats on his neck?" she said, describing him so I could remember.

"Oh yeah, the hood ass niggas. He was cute tho," I said remembering the night.

"Yeah, that's my boo," Briana giggled, while fumbling around in her purse until she found her mirror.

I rolled my eyes internally. Everybody was her boo. I'll admit, we both had the worst taste in men. We liked them hood and ninety percent of the time, they weren't worth shit. Only problem was, Briana could be naïve and most guys took advantage of her because of it. The crazy part was Briana was a very pretty girl. Although she had an athletic, it complimented her petite frame. She was brown skinned with golden highlights that made her light brown eyes glow. She reminded me a lot of Zoe Saldana.

Briana's main issue was she could be an airhead at times. Her lack of conversation, as well as her lack of motivation, didn't get her far with guys of quality. Nevertheless, that was my baby sister and I'd knock a bitch's head off for her.

"Well that's wassup. I gotta meet him one day soon," I said, lying. I had no interest whatsoever of meeting any of her so called "homeboys."

"I'm surprised you haven't yet. We be together most of the time," she said, while staring into her compact mirror and fixing her strip eyelashes.

"Oh yeah?" I laughed. "That's why ya ass be MIA, not answering the phone?"

"Whateva hoe, let's talk about you and Rashid." She took one more look at herself, closed the mirror, and stuffed it back in her purse. Briana was so self-absorbed.

"Definitely nothing to talk about there. I'm focused and I ain't worried about no nigga if his name ain't *Money*. Besides at this point, we have bigger fish to fry and don't have time to be bullshitting with niggas."

As soon as I made the comment Briana became irritated. She looked down and pretended to observe her polished blue nails.

"Whatever bitch. So wassup?" she asked jokingly, doing her best to conceal her light attitude.

Briana didn't like people judging her, especially me. She always thought I was trying to tell her she was fuckin up. That wasn't exactly the case, but at the moment, the last thing that should be on her mind was a broke, scheming ass nigga.

I decided to change the subject to keep the peace. Lord knows, I didn't feel like cursing her out today.

"I called you to meet me because I got another phone call this morning," I said seriously, getting down to business. We have until tomorrow to wire this money. They want a half million but that's definitely not happening. I figure we could stall them by giving them $50G's. I figure we would split it." It was more of a statement than a question.

I paused for Briana to respond. I was praying she had half of the fifty thousand. To many it would seem like small change compared to what we had made, however, like typical folk who weren't use to having anything, we ran through it like the speed of lightning.

"Aight, looks like we have no choice right," she responded casually.

Briana was one of those people who hid

their emotions very well. You would never be able to tell she was going through something until she snapped. Here we were being extorted and she comes in giggling about her new boyfriend. I on the other hand was the exact opposite. I engaged Briana in conversation to keep the peace. She was one of those people you had to accept for who they were and deal with on their terms, otherwise you'd always find yourself arguing and at odds. Being as though she was one of the very few family members I had, I often found myself biting my tongue and letting a lot of shit go unsaid.

"You're right. We really don't have a choice, however, what I'm worried about is, what if we pay them, and they don't stop. Then this shit will never end." I stared off, looking at nothing in particular.

Briana shifted around in the worn red booth. "I guess we'll just figure that out when the time comes. We can't really cry over spilt milk; just gotta do our best to clean it up. It's fucked up but we'll get through it. I'll have my money in the morning tho."

She glanced down at her vibrating phone on the table. I noticed her frequent peeks at her phone, so I figured I would wrap up our conversation.

"I'ma let you get back to ya boo. Plus it's after four, so I gotta make my way back to Willow Grove to pick up Layla from school."

I dropped an eight dollar tip on the table and rose up to give Briana a kiss on the cheek. We never received affection from adults as children, so we made up for it by giving it to one another.

"Aight boo, I'll meet up with you tomorrow then."

The drive to pick up Layla was longer than expected. There had been a fender bender and it was causing delays. I sucked my teeth and cursed in frustration. I had no choice but to grin and bear it. As I crawled through the midday traffic, I thought about wiring the money in the morning. What if things went wrong? What if it wasn't enough in the end? Even if we paid them the full amount, what if they still continued to black mail us?

No matter what we were going to lose. How bad we would lose, was the question. At lunch, Briana had insisted we tell Onney what was going on. She thought she may have some money to contribute to the payoff.

Of course she introduced the idea, but ultimately it wound up being me who would be assigned to deliver the bad news. At the rate things were going, it didn't really even matter how she took it. No matter how you look at things, what we had been doing was illegal.

After pondering for days, the only thing I had determined was we would need to file more phony returns to get the money the crook was looking for. I didn't have that type of money, nor was I giving up all that I had. The biggest problem we faced was that it was the end of March, and tax season was about to end. How the hell would we file over two hundred returns in two weeks? It was crunch time, and I prayed Briana and Onney were prepared.

I made it to Layla's school at 5:37. The after school program she was in let out at 5:30. I hated being late to pick up my angel. She saw me as soon as I pulled up. She was standing near the glass double doors at the entrance of the school. I waved to the teacher to confirm I was there for her.

Shortly after, Layla walked out with her round eyes beaming and her ponytails wagging. She skipped to the car carrying her Hello Kitty backpack. Her hair was slightly disheveled, and she looked like the typical messy nine year old with lunch stains on her uniform shirt. Despite all of that, she made my heart melt.

"Hey dollface." I leaned over to give her a kiss as she got into the car.

"Hey mommy. Why are you late?" she asked, with curiosity displayed on her pretty brown face.

"I'm sorry doll. The traffic was bad. I had met Auntie Briana for lunch and loss track of time."

"Oh. I thought you had forgot me," she said seriously, while fastening her seatbelt.

"Of course not silly, I would never forget you," I said.

"Well can you try to be on time tomorrow? A new Disney movie comes on tomorrow at six, and I need to have my homework done in time to see it. I missed the original premier, so I don't want to miss this showing."

I smiled and replied. "You got it. 5:30 sharp."

I shook my head. My daughter hardly had a care in the world. I made a vow that day that I would do everything necessary to ensure that it stayed that way.

After helping with homework and making dinner, I called Onney to let her know what was going on. Of course she took it the way I expected her to take it.

"So what happens now?" I heard her exhale a deep breath. She was whispering into the phone and sounded like she was moving around the house.

"Well, I'm gonna deposit $50,000 into the account they give me tomorrow. I'm gonna see if I can give them the other $450,000 after I file these returns."

"Damn Nina. Do you even have enough names left on the list to even file that many returns? With this kind of shit going on, there's no way I would think about trying to get more names out of the prison database. Who could be doing this? I don't have any enemies and I didn't tell anyone about this shit, not even my husband." She was still whispering and shuffling around in the house.

"I don't know. Briana and I talked about this the other day, and we couldn't come up with an answer. You know my circle is small, and I definitely don't go around telling anyone my business."

"Yeah. Well, what about Briana. She always had a big mouth, even when we were kids."

Onney and Briana never really cared much for one another. They weren't close and wouldn't be in contact if it wasn't for me. They were exact opposites, with Onney being work-orientated and quiet, and Briana outgoing and loud.

"True, but Briana knows the consequences behind this shit. She's not stupid."

Onney grew irritated at what she considered my naive attitude. "Bottom line is people are deceitful and someone who knows one of us is blackmailing us."

I shifted the phone to my other palm since the one I was using had grown sweaty. I was beginning to get irritated with my older sister. She surely had a lot to say with no money to contribute. However, Onney was right about what she way saying; someone we knew was blackmailing us. One thing for sure, whoever it was would have hell to pay when I found out. I hung up the phone with her and promised to call back the following night.

After hanging up the phone with Onney, I realized that Rashid was right, and we did need to talk. I needed his help. Ever since I was a child I was one of those people that did what they had to do, whether I wanted to or not. This was one of those times. I didn't like showing people that I was vulnerable, however, I had to be a woman and go to Rashid to let him know that I didn't have it all together at this point. It was extremely important for Rashid to understand that I needed him to be there for Layla.

I wasn't going to tell him exactly what was

going on, but I was going to let him know that I needed him. It wasn't the easiest task to be faced with, especially since I had literally just cursed him out and kicked him out of my house the other day.

The truth was, Rashid wasn't all that bad. He was one of those types that made all the wrong decisions for the right reasons. We had been young when we got together and he wasn't shit for a boyfriend, but he did really want his family to have. He had really tried to provide for us, even though he failed at it. Bottom line was, I needed to have a sit down with him.

It was 12am when Rashid knocked on the door. I sent him a text message earlier to see if he could come by so we could talk. He had just gotten off his 3-11 shift at a meat manufacturing company, and still had on his work clothes when he showed up. I let him in, but this time I had on sweat pants and a tank top.

"You hungry?" I asked, greeting him with a half-smile.

"Yeah, I am," he replied quickly.

I walked off to the kitchen to warm up some of the leftover Baked Ziti I had made earlier. I made small talk with Rashid while he ate, and then finally decided to approach the dreaded conversation about the situation I was in. I pulled out a chair and sat adjacent to him at the counter height dining set. I wasn't sure where to begin.

"Rashid, I called you here tonight because I have some shit going on my end. I can't really go into much details, but I need to know that if necessary, you will be there for Layla 100%. I stared at Rashid with a serious face.

He stopped eating and replied. "No doubt, but what's going on?"

"I can't really go into it too much, but I just need to know that you will be there for Layla and be a better father. I'm in a little bit of trouble and hopefully I can get out of it. The main thing for me is preparing for the worse, but hoping for the best. My primary concern is Layla's well-being if something happens to me.

Ultimately, you and I are all she has, and she depends on us.

"Whatever's going on with you, you don't have to tell me about it right now, but I will definitely be there for my daughter. And whenever you feel like talking about what's going on, or anything for that matter, I'm here. I know I haven't been the best, but those three years in prison changed me. I love yall, even though you may not believe it. And I'ma prove that."

I smiled. I knew he would at least try. At that moment, I remembered what had attracted me to him in the first place.

Rashid stood six feet tall, and was extremely handsome except for a long scar that went down the side of his light brown face. His eyes were round and had a darkness about them that hinted at a mysterious past. He had always been passionate and loving, even when he was doing wrong. I guess for those reasons, we fought hard and loved even harder. A girl like me could only take but so much though. He had been my everything, and sharing him was something I just could not do under any circumstances. Over time, with too many wrongs, and not enough rights, the love I had turned to resentment and eventually faded. Well, that's what I forced myself to feel anyway.

I switched my focus to clearing the table. Ignoring Rashid and sticking to my cold attitude kept me from getting sucked into his web. This particular night, however, it was hard to do. I was going through something, making me very vulnerable, so of course my attitude reflected that.

Without making eye contact, I told Rashid he was more than welcome to sleep in the guest bedroom since I knew he was tired, and probably didn't feel like driving back to North Philly.

"Towels and wash cloths are in the linen closet near the bathroom and the washer and dryer is near the back door," I told him.

"Aight cool. And thanks Nina. I just want us to be friends. On some real shit. I can't have it my way, so I'll take that rather that nothing at all. You a good chick for real and I fucked up. I was young, but I do appreciate you letting me make it up by being a better father to my daughter. Hopefully one day you'll give us another chance."

I smiled at his seemingly sincere revelation and walked off to get some rest.

FOUR

THE NEXT MORNING I was stressed to the max. Rashid had already dropped Layla off at school for me and went home to Germantown. I stayed home and sat in my bedroom to wait for "the" call. I had already told my blackmailer that I would not have a full half a million dollars. The money I would be depositing was in fact just that: a mere deposit. After staring at the phone for what seemed like an eternity, it finally rang. It was 11am and I had been waiting for almost two hours.

"Hello," I asked, speaking into the receiver.

"Do you have the money? If so I have the banking information for you and your sister to make the deposit."

"I have $50,000," I blurted out. There was no need beating around the bush with the bullshit. This was serious shit, and I needed to know right then and there if they would take it or not.

"When will you have the rest?" the muffled voice asked. I could never tell if it was a male or female.

"I need until May, and I also need your word that this will be done and over with. I will agree to your terms, but I need this to be over once we pay you."

"Done. But if you try to burn me, I'll ruin you. Understand?"

"I understand," I replied solemnly.

The caller gave me all the information I needed to make the deposit into the Bank of America account, so I headed over to Briana's house in the Mt. Airy section of Philadelphia.

When I pulled up to Briana's I noticed there was a blue, late model Chevy Monte Carlo parked in the driveway. It had tinted windows and screamed "Pull me over!" I figured it was her little jump off Eric, and I was pissed that she was more worried about being laid up, sucking dick, rather than answering her damn phone for something important. I had been calling the bitch all morning.

I banged on the door for several minutes until she answered it. The sight of her pissed me off further, especially because she wasn't dressed, and she already knew she was supposed to go with me to make the deposit at the bank.

"Yo what the fuck?" I asked frowning, as she opened the door to let me in, which she seemed hesitant to do.

"My fault, I overslept, let me go get some clothes on." She proceeded to run back to the room in nothing but panties and bra set, showing off her small curves.

I couldn't believe she could oversleep on something as important as this. She was acting like shit wasn't serious, and I made a mental note to check her ass when I got the opportunity.

"Hurry up," I said to her, as she walked off

to get dressed.

Just as Briana was turning the corner to her bedroom, I heard another voice, which indicated that she did indeed have company. Being nosey, I pretended I was going to the bathroom, but was nearly knocked over by Briana's thug ass boyfriend. In all actuality I bumped into him not paying attention, however, I was still agitated.

"Damn--My bad," I stammered, apologizing.

"Damn sis, you sleep?" he asked jokingly, displaying a set of perfect white teeth.

I laughed lightly, and responded. "Naa. Long morning, and need to get going. You must be Eric?" I asked.

Eric was actually handsome in a rough and rugged kind of way. He rocked a set of fuzzy cornrows on his head and had a handsome face with a strong jawline. Looking at him, I did in fact remember him from the casino that night. I could see why Briana was head over heels for him. He was the typical good-looking, bad boy that she always fell for.

"Yep, Yep. Nice to meet you," he replied.

"Well I'm Nina," I said, forcing a smile on my face.

I was pretty sure he knew who I was, but figured it was polite to introduce myself. I really didn't care to make small talk but found it unavoidable since I had nearly knocked him over in the hallway. Just then, Briana turned the corner and saved me from the forced conversation.

"I see you two have met. You ready?" She looked at me as she smoothed her hair back, and pulled an elastic band on it to secure it into a neat ponytail. Brushing her clothes off, she was now ready to go.

"Yeah, I'm ready," I replied.

The ride to the bank was quiet since I was still irritated with Briana. She didn't take shit seriously. On top of that she only had $20,000 and not the half of the money that we had originally agreed on. Because of her, I had to go out of the way to my own bank, and take another $5,000 out of my personal savings account.

I honestly felt like I was going through this whole ordeal alone. I was focusing most of my time on dealing with the blackmailer, running behind Briana, and reasoning with Onney. On top of that I was working, being a mom, and managing my properties. The nail bar had been put on hold for now, but I was beginning to get overwhelmed.

"Nina watch out!" Briana yelled out, suddenly.

I slammed on the breaks so hard, our bodies jerked forward and you could hear the tires screech. A group of teenagers had dashed across the road trying to catch the bus and had almost become road-kill. They continued across the street while giving me dirty looks. Briana was still perched forward in her seat, with her right hand clenching the door.

"Yo what's wrong with you? You're spaced the fuck out!" she yelled, with a bewildered look on her face.

I smacked my teeth in anger and irritation. "Nah, I'm stressed the fuck out, and nobody is making it any damn better." I was about two seconds from slapping fire out her ass.

"Motherfuckers is extorting us for a quarter million dollars apiece and you're more worried about chasing dick, rather than dealing with the issue. Onney's no fucking help and doesn't have a damn dime to put up. And ya ass stay coming up short on everything but always got a new purse on ya arm. So if anybody spaced the fuck out, it's you. You need a reality check, cuz clearly you not in tune to what the fuck is happening."

Briana responded in a lowered tone, carefully choosing her words. "I am in tune. I just handle stress differently from you, but I'm going through something just like you. And Eric is not just dick I'm chasing. He's my man. That's your choice that you choose not to seek comfort from anyone."

"Seek comfort? Briana, you don't just go around telling people you're being blackmailed. That's something you, Onney and I should be dealing with together."

"That's not what I'm saying Nina. I said *seek comfort*, not *confide*."

"Whatever. You need to be more active in coming up with a fucking solution. It's always me trying to figure things out and hold shit together. You just make sure you're present when it's time to get the other $450,000. We have to file several hundred returns to get that kind of money, and we only have until May to do it."

Briana snapped her neck back and looked at me crazily. "May? You can't be serious. How are we going to file that many returns? We usually do that over 3 months."

"My point exactly," I said, hoping she now realized that we would basically be working non-stop and trying to pull off a miracle.

I made the turn on Broad Street, and pulled the car into the Bank of America parking lot. Briana and I made our way into the bank and quickly made the deposit. Since it was still early, the line wasn't too long. Once the deposit was made, I sent out the text to confirm the transaction was done. Within two minutes I got a text that confirmed it was received.

Briana and I sat quietly in thought on the way home. I informed her that the tax filing would begin tomorrow, and that I needed her focused and present so we could get the money we needed. It took weeks for tax refunds to come back, and we had two weeks at the most to file several hundred returns. We had to make sure all of them were error free so they wouldn't be delayed. We had our work cut out for us. Between my work schedule and managing repairs on my properties, I expected to pull some all-nighters.

Later that night I thought about what Briana had said, and she did have a little bit of a point. I didn't have to go at the stress of my situation completely alone. Even though I had no man, I could silently find comfort within my friendships. I decided to call up my girlfriend Asia. With everything that had been going on, I hadn't spoken to her in like a week.

Asia had two kids and happened to be putting one to sleep when I called, so we spoke briefly. However, we did make plans to meet up on Saturday for drinks. After speaking with her I called Onney. Surprisingly, she answered on the first ring.

"Hey Nina," she said, sounding wide

awake.

"Hey. You busy?" I asked.

"Naa. Why wassup?"

"I just wanna talk is all. It's a lot of pressure from this whole situation, and I'm starting to get frustrated. Just wanna vent."

For a half an hour, I expressed my frustration with Briana, her lack of focus, and how I felt she wasn't taking the situation seriously. It was almost as if her mind was occupied on something else completely. Ever since she had met this guy Eric, it was as if her world became consumed around him, and it was proving harder and harder for me to get in contact with her.

After venting, Onney relieved some of her own frustrations she had pent up. Her and her husband had been having problems for years and had been even more at odds the past couple of months. He drank and had a gambling problem. For almost a year, she had been handling the bills solely on her income, while he gambled his away at the casino. She revealed that when he won big, he was generous and kind, but when he lost he was mean and drowned himself in alcohol. He still worked, but that too was in jeopardy because inmates were complaining about his aggression. More recently, he had begun questioning her finances after she leased a new car because her old one was giving her problems.

"Nina, truthfully, I'm at my wits end. The mortgage is killing me, and the money I was getting with yall was keeping me afloat. I don't know how much longer I can deal with this shit with Kevin.

"I don't know Onney… But if it makes you feel any better, I'm here if you need any help financially. I made some investments and I'm okay for now…Well, if everything plays out right with this situation anyway. My main concern is, what will you do over time? Clearly, we can't do this scheme anymore after we get this money to pay this person off. I mean, if your mortgage is too much, and Kevin isn't helping, you may need to try to sell and downsize."

"I thought about that. It's other shit too. It's just a lot." She paused.

Clearly she had some bigger issues going on in that house. I made a vow to myself that day that I would be a bigger part of Onney's life. Even when we were split up as kids, she went through that ordeal alone, unable to confide in her sisters. I wanted her to know that she always had me, and that if I could help, I would.

I later ended the call with a newfound appreciation for my sister, as well as relationships in general. You never knew what a person was going through and I was always so quick to judge.

FIVE

THE WEEK THAT followed was hectic just like I expected. My schedule at Aetna was 7a-3p, but I was working until nearly seven in the evening because of my properties. The repairs to my two rooming houses were finally done, so I had been focused on getting the rooms rented. The remainder of my afternoon consisted of meeting with potential renters, getting keys made, and running back and forth to the bank to make deposits. Layla was staying at the daycare until seven so I could handle business. By the time I got home, took a shower and made a quick pasta skillet dinner, I was beat.

Briana would meet me at 9pm so we could work on filing returns for six hours. We were on a tight schedule, and had been working 30 hours per week to meet our deadline. I would sleep when we were done, and be back up at 5 am to get ready for work and drop Layla off at daycare. I had begun relying on caffeine to help me stay awake. Lately, Briana and I had become a bit distant. I was never the one to hate on anyone's happiness but lately she had been more of a sucker for love. She had been really chipper despite the predicament that we were in. Although finding it odd, I never said anything to her until she crossed the line.

It was Friday and I was waiting on Briana to show up to help me with returns. She was late but I decided to let it ride. That is until she showed up to my home with her boyfriend. When I looked out the window and saw a man behind the wheel of her BMW I saw red. Before Briana could open the door I was on her ass.

"Bitch I know damn well you didn't bring that fuck ass nigga to my house?" I asked, looking at Briana like she'd lost her mind. I walked around her and looked out the window to confirm I was correct. Sure enough, it was Eric.

"He dropped me off, what you trippin for?" she said, looking confused.

"I don't give a fuck who you fuck wit, but I don't want none of them broke, scheming ass niggas from North Philly at my house. You don't fuckin know him for-real Briana. Damn, you do some dumb ass shit." I said through clenched teeth, before walking off in aggravation.

Instead of walking away and letting me vent, Briana decided to follow behind me and argue.

"You know what Nina, you always got ya fuckin nose stuck in the air like you better than everybody else. You don't know him, and that's my dude so I don't see what the problem is. And besides, you act like Rashid ghetto, drug-dealing ass aint from North Philly."

Ignoring the statement about Rashid, I responded harshly. "I don't give a fuck who he is. He isn't my man! He's your temporary nigga. Every time I turn around you got a new nigga. I don't want none of them around me, or around the place that I plan to permanently rest my head with my daughter. Hood niggas like that pick air-head bitches like you to use, and they see you coming from a mile away. As you can see he left his punk ass Monte Carlo in North Philly and is pushing your fuckin BMW instead. Niggas be leeches, and I could see it when we was at the casino. That's why I turned my fuckin head when the nigga was giving me the eye."

As soon as those words came out, I regretted saying it. I had a major problem with the way I communicated sometimes. However, by the time I realized what I said was wrong, it was too late.

Not to be conceited but I regularly received attention, especially from hood ass niggas like Eric. I damn sure wasn't Beyoncé, but I was still a bad bitch. Unlike Briana, I was thick from top to bottom. Thighs, hips, everything curvy and swollen. When Briana's boyfriend and his friends walked by us, they of course did a double take. We were both fly that night, but the whole time, her lame ass boyfriend Eric

SHONTAIYE

was eyeing me like a piece of meat. Of course I'm about dollas, so I had no time to converse. Briana, of course took the bait, and that's why she was sitting there with the pissed face, mad because I was stating facts.

"You know what bitch, fuck you," she spat. "You can do this shit by yourself. I'ma call my man to pick me up, while you sit ya lonely, miserable ass in here by yaself. Maybe Rashid will come over and make you happy by fuckin ya sad raggedy ass."

I laughed out loud, but I was pissed at the comment. "Yeah, I don't have to beg niggas to fuck me. As a matter of fact I could probably have ya man eating out the palm of my hand or eating from *anywhere* for that matter. Trust me."

Before I could say anything else, Briana hauled off and punched me upside my head and then proceeded to grab a handful of my $400 weave. *Was this bitch crazy?*

Briana landed a couple blows to my back while I used my body weight to keep from tumbling over the couch, since we were still in the living room. She had my long hair pulled down, wrapped around her hand in a death grip. Once I was able to regain my balance and had one foot planted firmly, I swung hard and punched her in the side. I didn't want to hurt her but I wanted her to get the fuck off of me. The blow did exactly what I hoped it would do, make her lose her breath and let go of my damn hair. When she let go I rushed her, slammed her against the door and grabbed her collar.

"What the fuck is wrong with you bitch? I'll fuck you up!" I yelled, as I violently shook her against the hard cherry wood door.

"On some real shit, call ya nigga so you can get the fuck out my house! You got me fucked up disrespecting me in my own home!"

Spittle flew from my mouth as I released her with a shove and walked off enraged. *I couldn't believe she would attack me over a lame ass nigga.* I knew Briana was feeling dude, but for her to go against me, it had to be serious. We were too close for that. This stupid ass argument had gotten out of control.

I went to my room and slammed my door. My fist were clenched at my sides while I paced back and forth around the room, trying to catch my breath, and regain my composure. It was taking all of me to keep from going back in the living room and laying hands on her ass. I heard Briana yelling to Eric on her cell phone for him to come get her before she "fucks me up."

I paid her no mind since it would be a cold day in hell before she whooped my ass. The bitch had gotten lucky with the couple punches she did get. I weighed way more than her, and was a lot quicker with my hands,

so things could have gotten ugly very quickly if she wasn't my baby sister.

After about ten minutes I went to check on Layla to make sure she was still sleep. Somehow she had managed to rest through the commotion. I'm glad she was a heavy sleeper. I would have hated for her to see me and her aunt fighting like that. Briana and I had our share of fights in our life, but this one seemed different. We were seriously drifting apart and it was all behind a damn man.

The next morning I woke up feeling like shit. I had dozed off on the couch, and hadn't even bothered to wrap my hair. Briana had pulled one of my tracks loose, and my head was throbbing. *Stupid bitch,* I thought. I went to my master bathroom and looked in the mirror. I didn't have a bruise from the punch Briana landed on my face, but I damn sure looked a mess. I rummaged around in my medicine cabinet until I found my purple wig brush. I wrapped my disheveled hair and proceeded to slather on my green mint julep mask. I swore by that mask since I was a teenager. It was cheap as hell, but it got the job done.

It was Saturday so I figured I would relax most of the afternoon and then take Layla to her dad. He was off on the weekends and had a small apartment in Germantown. I didn't like the area but I wouldn't deny Layla the quality time she spent with her father. I envied the adoration she displayed for him.

Two o clock rolled around quicker than I had anticipated, and I found myself struggling to get motivated to get out of the house and in route to Germantown.

"Layla do you have your bag ready?" I asked.

"Yes mommm," she responded, dragging *mom* in a whiney tone.

"What's wrong with you?" I asked, noticing that her normal jovial attitude had been replaced with a somber one.

"Nothing," she replied. I wasn't buying it. Something was up, and I was going to get to the bottom of it.

"Layla, if something is wrong, you know you can tell me right. No matter what it is, you can come to me. So what's going on? I know you, and I can tell when you're unhappy."

She hesitated a second, and then her sad demeanor switched to a warmer one.

"Well, I normally like going to my dad's, but he has a new girlfriend and she be over his house a lot. I don't really get to spend as much time with him anymore when I go over there. She has two boys, and they're kinda bad. They fight, and I don't really like being around them. Do I have to go today? I'd rather stay home and be with you."

I grew angry as my daughter explained the situation to me. Here I was doing my best to raise her with minimal stress in her life, and Rashid's ass was doing the opposite. His dumb ass was playing house with some hood-rat, while he was supposed to be spending quality time with his daughter.

"Did one of them hit you?" I asked. My primary concern was that she had not been struck by anyone in that damn house. If she said yes, it would be Desert Storm for everybody over that bitch when I got there.

"No. My dad doesn't let them do any fighting around me."

"Good. Cuz ya dad know I don't play. And of course you can stay home honey. I'll talk to your dad and let him know how you feel and that you want to stay home for the weekend. He won't be upset."

I thought about texting Rashid but I figured he would just try to lie about it and that would further piss me off. I would call him later and discuss the issue; for now I would focus on cheering my baby up.

I called Asia to see if she wanted to join me

and Layla at Dave and Buster's with her kids. Our girls night out had been canceled since Layla decided to stay home, but I figured we could still do something while incorporating our children. I offered to pay for everything since I knew that she was having some financial difficulties. Although she made a good salary at Aetna, her husband wasn't working and was having trouble finding a job.

Asia took me up on my offer, so later that evening we met up at Dave and Busters on Christopher Columbus Boulevard in Philly. She of course, brought along her adorable twin boys, Trevor and Tyler. Asia and I had margaritas and hot wings, while the kids ran around the arcade, only returning to get more money for their game cards.

"So what's been going on girl?" Asia asked. "You be MIA at Aetna."

"Girl, I still be working." I laughed. "I just finished repairing a couple properties down in North Philly. So far I have four. I got them for dirt cheap because they were shells, but it's been very time consuming and labor intensive to fix them up." I didn't like getting to detailed about my side ventures.

Although Asia was my friend, she had a big mouth and was nosey at times. Asia was mixed with black and white, and had a face full of freckles. She wasn't very attractive, with small lips, big eyes, and a head full of reddish curls. However, what Asia lacked in looks she made up for in personality. She was very bubbly, loving and warm; like another sister.

"Damn, that's wassup. I didn't know you had properties. But you've always been good with your money, saving and shit. I'm about to really start saving more; as soon as my income tax check come back. With two kids and Drew not working, I'm supposed to get back a nice amount.

Asia's comment about taxes caught me off guard. As much as I loved her, that comment quickly ended the warm and fuzzy thoughts I was just having about her. I quickly grew uncomfortable and began to silently question why she would bring up income taxes. I was one of those people who wore their emotions on their sleeve, well in my case, my face, so I quickly excused myself to run to the bathroom. When I returned I was calm but made a mental note to be a lot more observant of the small circle I kept. I also decided to get off the subject of money and taxes, and talk about something else.

When I thought about the people close to me, I noticed that many of them were having money problems; Onney, Asia, and even Briana. At the thought of Briana, I looked down at my phone for the tenth time that day to see if she had called or texted me. Of course she still hadn't called and I began to wonder if maybe I went a little overboard with the comment about her boyfriend. Briana had always been a little jealous type, so the comment probably pissed her insecure ass off to the max.

After talking with Asia about the incident, she confirmed that I had went overboard with my comment and I owed Briana an apology. That still didn't excuse her for hitting me in my house, but like Asia said, why make a remark like that about her boyfriend who she clearly cares for.

"Imagine her saying that about Rashid," Asia said, trying to rationalize the situation.

"Girl please. I wouldn't care, but I do see what you're saying." I agreed with her to a certain extent.

"Then you also have to take into consideration that Briana really looks up to you. I've only met her a few times but I could tell she does. She obviously wishes she was more like you and when you made that comment you probably triggered jealousy and insecurities from within her. Just call her and apologize. You were wrong for saying what you said, and her attacking you was purely emotional and stemmed from that situation."

"I guess you're right. But that still don't mean she can just haul off hitting people, pulling up my damn tracks and shit."

Asia burst out laughing when I said that. I admit, I had to laugh too.

After finding and gathering our worn out kids, we parted ways. I texted Asia on the way home, thanking her for her insight. I valued our friendship since she was one of the ones who kept it real all the time. She probably knew me better than even Briana did. Nevertheless, I was still being blackmailed by someone close to me, so I would still continue to limit and monitor certain conversation. However, I think it was really time to start talking to Briana about what she may have said drunkenly to one of her girlfriends.

Even though Briana and I were inseparable when we were young, she always had a ton of friends. She was outgoing while I was more quiet and analytical. Although we were both pretty, she was the more charismatic one. That was something I secretly envied. Even as an adult, she oftentimes would have gatherings at her house and invite five or six close girlfriends. I would always opt out, since I had nothing in common with the bar hopping bitches she hung around.

It was becoming more and more likely that one of Briana's friends was probably the culprit. Briana only worked on and off, but had a nice row home in the Mt. Airy section of Philadelphia. Anyone not familiar with that section, should know that it's one of the better neighborhoods for African American's in the city. Certain parts of Mt. Airy is home to teachers, doctors and executives. I'm sure many of her friends were curious as to what she did to afford her the ability to live there, as well as drive a new BMW.

By the time I pulled up to my driveway, Layla was leaning over in the back seat sleep. A trail of spit went from her face to the seat of my Mustang as she tossed in her sleep. Dave and Busters had worn my baby out. I shook her awake and helped her walk drunkenly into the house. I didn't bother her with undressing since she slept in spurts. I figured she could bathe and brush her teeth in an hour or so when she woke up. I used the opportunity to walk outside and call Rashid. He had been calling and texting me about when I was bringing Layla since earlier in the afternoon.

"Hey Rashid. We need to talk." I figured I would use a calmer approach with this situation. I didn't know how serious he was with the chick or if he knew how uncomfortable Layla was, so I wanted to have facts before I reacted.

"Yeah wassup, and why didn't you bring Layla? I've been texting and calling you all day."

"Yeah I saw that, but who's the chick with the bad ass kids you have around the house when Layla is there?" I asked. Aggravation oozed from my voice.

"Who Kiana? That's just a shorty I was poppin. Before you flip out tho Nina, let me explain what's going on first..." Rashid spoke fast, since he knew I was about to let him have it.

"I already know how you feel about females being around Layla, cuz truthfully I don't want any nigga around her on ya end. However, she and I are just friends and we aren't serious. She's actually about to get the fuck out. Shorty lost her place a couple weeks ago. Got evicted or something. I was doing her a favor. She got them two boys, so I felt sorry for her. She asked me, and I told her she could stay here a week or so until she figured something out. I'm not there like that anyway since I work all the time, and I figured by the time I get there they'll be sleep. I didn't think shit through as far as how it would affect Layla and our weekends together. That is where I fucked up, and I apologize to you, and I will definitely apologize to Layla. Shorty is a bum bitch on some real shit, and she gon take them bad ass kids and get out. I would never put anyone before my daughter."

I paused before responding, since I was pissed off.

"First of all I know you ain't talking about Kiana that used to live around 10th and Diamond? Booter sister?" I asked, already knowing the answer.

"Yeah," he responded, slightly embarrassed because of her reputation.

"I just seen her ass a couple days ago at the Willow Grove mall, probably stealing. Ya trifling ass a trip," I commented.

Booter was an acquaintance of Rashid's. He was a hood ass nigga with a hoe ass sister. She wasn't pretty by a long shot, and only had ass and tits going for her. She was a hood-rat with no desire for an education and lived month to month by fucking, sucking, and living off welfare and S.S.I checks.

"Rashid you have no idea how sad and uncomfortable you made Layla feel. She doesn't know that hoe or her fuckin kids. On top of that, she said the bitch's son's fight, which is no surprise since they mother is Kiana. Luckily they didn't hit her. What if she had gotten hurt? She didn't even want to go over there today," I said, adding salt to the wound. He sat quietly on the phone, so I continued.

"You really need to use your head when you make decisions. What if I told you that she can't go over there anymore and your visits would be monitored?" I asked.

He sucked his teeth and the volume in his voice rose. "Then you'd be on some bullshit," he stated, ignoring everything else I had just said.

"I'd be on some bullshit because you had a hood-rat around our fucking child. It's about respect Rashid! Respect your daughter, and respect her mother!" I shouted, losing my patience.

Realizing that I was in front of my house in

an affluent community, I lowered my voice. I didn't want anyone in my business or thinking I was some big mouthed, ghetto black girl.

"Yo, I already said I fucked up. Goddamn. What the fuck else you want me to say? I definitely aint gon sit on the phone and argue with you. That's for damn sure."

"You know what Rashid. Go the fuck to work and save ya money for a lawyer. Cuz ya ass gon need it when I file for sole custody."

"You on some nut shit Nina!" he accused, while yelling into the phone.

"Every decision I make, I analyze how it'll affect our daughter. You just admitted that you don't. Until you change that and start putting her first, then you won't see her. Matter of fact, you can see her. In a public place, supervised. My lawyer will make sure of that," I threatened.

Rashid paused and then spoke harshly. "You know what Nina, fuck you! On some real shit. You on some corny shit and karma is a bitch."

I hung up the phone in his ear just as he was about to continue his verbal tirade. I didn't give a damn what he said or what he thought. He was out of line for taking Layla to his home to play house with a bitch and her kids. I don't care what the situation was.

Here he was, coming over here professing his love for me in front of Layla, and then taking her to his home where he has a woman and her kids living. That shit was probably confusing as fuck to her. He was setting bad examples for his young, highly impressionable daughter. That's why females were settling for anything these days. They were constantly being shown and taught that it was normal. Additionally, I was pissed about him fucking hoe ass Kiana.

We would both calm down later, and I would call him so we could set up a better arrangement for him to spend time with Layla. However, from now on she would not be going to his home. At the end of the day Rashid wasn't retarded. He knew he was wrong, and he would see it from my perspective with a clear head.

◇◇◇

Hours later, I sat relaxing by my bay window. This was by far, my favorite feature of my home. Plush pillows and cushions aligned the seating space, while expensive purple and gold drapes adorned the large windows. This was my space to read, think, and reflect.

I picked up my phone for the millionth time and checked to see if I had any missed calls. I had several from Rashid, but none from Briana. I decided it was now or never, so I dialed her number to apologize about what I had said. After the second ring, she answered. Knowing Briana, she probably was waiting for "that" call just like I had been.

"Hello?" she answered dryly.

"Hey," I responded. I took an exaggerated deep breath so she would understand that what I was doing was not easy.

"Listen, I know you're probably still mad at me, but at the end of the day we are family. What I said was wrong. I shouldn't have said it. I talked to Asia, and she said the same thing. I didn't mean the shit, but during the heat of the moment, I had to say something to get under your skin. So I apologize for that. I understand why you reacted the way you did, but it doesn't take away from the fact that I am your sister, and you can't just go around attacking people." I waited for her to respond. Ten seconds went by with no response from her. I grew nervous at the thought of rejection.

"Thank you," she said in a sincere tone, surprising me.

"I appreciate the fact that you called and apologized. I look up to you Nina. You're my big sister. I feel like you pass judgment on me a lot. I'm not perfect, and it just seems like you are so quick to let me know that. So you calling me apologizing, and saying you were wrong is very dear to me," Briana professed.

"I do apologize for hitting you. That wasn't the right way to handle it. I'm sorry...Like I said before, I handle stress different from you and I just snapped. You've been coming down on me hard lately with criticism and it's tough. But I do apologize for my actions, and I just want things to be back to normal."

I agreed and we ended the call with our

own set of promises. Briana promised to be more present while we handled our "situation," and I promised to be less critical and more understanding. After talking to Briana I felt bad. Was I this miserable "hard ass" type of person? Was I really being the "Negative Nancy" no one wanted to be around? That was who I did not want to be. Wasn't I happy? Or was I?

Later that night I found myself wide awake in bed, still pondering over my happiness and future. After all the drinking from Dave and Buster's earlier, plus my nightly wine ritual, I was running to and from the bathroom. As I walked across the plush carpet on my way to my private bath I decided to peek in on Layla. Peering around my home puzzled, I detected a foul odor in the air. I frowned at the stench.

I went to the kitchen and used my foot to press down on my stainless steel, no touch, trash can. When it opened I cringed from the smell of half eaten cheese dip from Dave and

Busters. I immediately began gathering it to take it out back to the dumpster behind my home. I ran to the room and got some sandals before I grabbed the trash.

Opening the door wide, I walked to the back of my yard where I kept the dumpster. After throwing the bag on the side, I turned around and was met by a dark, hooded figure who knocked me hard to the ground. *Thud!* My body jerked as I landed hard on my ass.

Hovering in front of me, the man leaned in to say something but I quickly scurried back to try to get away. My sandals slid off my feet and I suddenly felt my back hit the dumpster. There was nowhere to run. I wouldn't allow myself to scream, for if I did I would put Layla in immediate danger also. I didn't want her hearing me and then running out.

My heart pounded rapidly in my chest as shock ripped through my body. The intruder used his gloved hand to cover my mouth. With his free hand he grabbed my neck and applied enough pressure to cause me to immediately gasp for air. At that moment, fear cloaked me as I realized I was staring in the face of death. I was going to die right outside in my backyard by the trash, like a stray animal. All I could think of was my daughter Layla searching for me and finding me like this in the morning. Tears welled up in my eyes and made their way down my face.

The masked man suddenly loosened his grip some, and leaned into my ear really close to speak.

"I'm here to deliver a message and reminder for you and your sister. The half a million is still due soon. No funny shit. You're easily touchable, *any* and *everywhere*. If you scream or call the police, you'll die next time."

He quickly released, and backed away slowly, before cutting through my neighbor's home, and quickly disappearing into the darkness. The message he brought was very clear; this situation wasn't a game, and whoever was the person behind this, wanted their money as promised. I don't understand why they felt the need to use that type of fear and intimidation to get their point across. Just the thought of going to jail was enough to get us rattled by itself. Whatever the case was, I

SHONTAIYE

had one more week left to get the money, no matter what it took.

SIX

MONDAY WAS BACK around, and it was week two of our rapid tax filing spree. Things were still chaotic but weren't as bad as the previous week. I was still working my day job, however, I had rented all of my vacant rooms, out so I wasn't running all around Philadelphia behind potential tenants. I had been looking at a couple more large houses to purchase in the Germantown section, however, I would wait before I plunked down money I might later need. Additionally, making many of the homes livable required a great deal of time that I just didn't have at the moment.

SHONTAIYE

Throughout all of the adversity in my life, I still kept my sights on one day owning dozens of rental properties in the city. Once I reached that goal, I would branch out and start attacking other forms of real estate, like office buildings and complexes.

Briana was alone and on time tonight, so we were able to get started promptly. I didn't tell her or Onney about what had happened the previous night with the intruder. The whole incident had me extremely fearful and very cautious. I figured I would carry that burden alone so they both could at least sleep through the night. I also told myself that as soon as this was over, I would be selling my beloved townhouse and moving to a gated community where shit like that would never happen.

We had half of the two hundred refunds done and were right on schedule to have the other hundred done by the end of the week. With that being said, my fingers ached from typing, and my eyes were constantly red and tingling from lack of sleep.

With some minor manipulations on the tax

forms, we were able to get higher returns on many of them. The adjustments would allow us to see around $600-$700Gs. We planned to pay off the other four fifty and pocket the rest. This would be our last run, so we had to make it count for something.

"So Briana what do you plan to do after this?" I asked, just making small talk.

"Girl, I don't know. I'll probably take $30,000 and finally pay for hair school," she said, still focused on the laptop screen.

Briana had been doing weaves since we were teenagers. She wasn't the best braider but that was something she knew could be learned.

"Awesome," I responded, in a surprised manner. I was actually surprised that she had been considering going back to school for something.

"You'll do great with that. You know ya curls always be on point. Get that braiding down and you'll kill em in Philly on the weave tip."

Philly was known as the hair mecca of the country. Bitches lived and died for weaves and braids. It was common to see a chick at the bus stop with a $300-$400 weave. Females would buy a weave before they put the money towards a computer or car. Senseless, but nevertheless it was done.

"And you know I got ya back financially if you decide to open a shop...I ain't rich, but I got a lil sumn put up to the side where I could comfortably help you out."

Briana smiled brightly. "Thanks Nina. I'll definitely take you up on that offer. I already know what I'ma call it...*Baddies*, short for "Bad Bitches," she laughed.

I rolled my eyes and laughed while responding. "Only you would name a salon some dumb ghetto shit like that," I joked.

"Oh! Guess who I seen! I forgot to tell you," she revealed excitedly.

"Mommy's sister, Aunt Sheena. She was cleaned up and working at McDonald's, down Broad and Allegheny."

"Broad and Allegheny? Why were you way down there?" I frowned. "Well whatever, how was she?"

I quickly reminded myself that my protective, inquisitive ways could come across as overbearing and critical so I stopped myself when asking why Briana was way the fuck down Allegheny. Here we were almost thirty years old and I was questioning her about her whereabouts like a kid. I had to stop doing that.

"I was with Eric. He live in North Philly remember? We had sat down to eat and she was working the counter. She looked so good. She had some fake teeth in and she had gained weight and everything. As a matter of fact, I gave her my number and I'ma pick her up tomorrow when she gets off. She say she been at a half-way house and had been locked up for five years. I pray she stay straight. I would love to have her around. She remind me so much of mommy. You should come by with Layla."

I wasn't sure what to think of reconnecting with Aunt Sheena. A part of me felt like I should be angry because we were in and out of foster homes while she was running around getting high. However, another part of me, the grown up part of me, understood that she had an addiction that she couldn't control.

I agreed to go by Briana's and see Aunt Sheena. I would not bring up the past. What happened, happened, and I would only move forward. I had been trying to apply that concept to every aspect of my life, including with Rashid.

The day after our argument I spoke with him. He agreed that if he every decided to get serious with someone he would discuss it with me before Layla met her. The same would go for me. Rashid however, insisted that would never be the case, because we would eventually get back together. Highly unlikely, but I was no fortune teller so I just let him talk.

The next day, I pulled up to Briana's house around 6:15. I had just picked Layla up from school and made a pit stop to the supermarket so Layla could make a salad at the salad bar. I hated when she ate in my car, but my baby was hungry so she would not be deprived.

I didn't see Briana's car in the yard, so I called her to make sure she was home. She answered on the first ring.

"Hey Nina! We're in the house. The door is open."

"Ok cool, where's your car?" I asked.

She paused. "Oh, Eric has it. His is in the shop," she lied.

"Ok ok, boo. Well we're coming in now."

I hung up the phone and rolled my eyes. I told Briana that the nigga Eric was a leech. There probably wasn't shit wrong with his car. He was probably riding around frauding and flossing in her BMW like it was his shit. Hopefully he won't tear her shit up. The last car she had, an all-white 2013 Dodge Charger, had been wrecked by a former boyfriend.

We walked into Briana's home and Layla greeted her with a warm hug. She adored Briana and I wished Briana would spend more time with her. Aunt Sheena sat in the dining area and stood up nervously to greet us. She had tears in her eyes and appeared anxious but happy, like she just found her long lost family member. In reality, she actually had.

"Ooo my goodness," she gushed. "You look exactly the same. Still beautiful, but all grown up," she exclaimed emotionally, before reaching out her large arms to embrace me.

I opened my arms to give her a hug. She reminded me so much of my mother. The physical resemblance was uncanny. Aunt Sheena was full-figured just like my mother. Even though she had been on drugs all those years, she never became extremely skinny like most addicts. The woman standing before me looked good. She had all her weight back and looked well put together, with false teeth, and her hair neatly curled under.

"Hey Aunt Sheena. I'm so happy to see you. We missed you."

Emotions overwhelmed me and I quickly realized how much I missed having a mother figure in my life. I hoped to get that back with Aunt Sheena. Lord knows we all needed her in our life. I looked to my side and Briana was crying silent tears. We were all so happy.

Aunt Sheena got acquainted with everyone while we played catch up and ate some wing dings Briana had made. Aunt Sheena quickly took to Layla, continuously hugging her and pinching her cheeks. Our visit was very emotional, yet happy. However, it was cut short because Aunt Sheena had to be back at the half-way house by 9. Since Eric wasn't back yet, we all piled up in my Mustang and I dropped her off.

The whole time Briana was constantly calling Eric to see where he was. Of course he wasn't answering, and when he finally did he claimed he wasn't getting good reception and had been tied up. I pretended not to notice. These days it was better for me to just mind my business. I didn't want to get punched again.

We all said bye to Aunt Sheena while we exchanged numbers, promising to keep in touch. I had every intention of doing so. With her being straight, she gave off such a warm motherly vibe that I desperately needed. Time would tell whether she stayed straight or not, however, after five years in prison you would think that she would. I could only go off of

The week was going by smoothly and things

were looking up. I had only been contacted once from our blackmailer about the money. For some reason the voice sounded a little different from last time. Maybe my mind was playing tricks on me.

Aunt Sheena was still coming around after work and had been keeping in contact with everyone via phone calls and texts daily, sometimes multiple times a day. Briana was even considering inviting her to come live with her after she got out of the half-way house in a few months.

Even though things were going smoothly, I still was extra tired. More so, because Briana hadn't been feeling well lately. She would go to the bathroom multiple times while we were working and complained of stomach and headaches. I prayed to God she wasn't pregnant by that fool Eric. I had let her go home twice, and I just stayed up later to make up for her not being there. I would be glad when all this shit was over. I typically didn't require a lot of sleep, but lately I was truly deprived, running off a couple of hours.

Later during the week while I was working

at Aetna, Asia stopped to talk to me at my desk.

"Hey Nina. You been alright lately?" she asked, appearing a bit concerned.

"I'm good girl. Just been running around lately and haven't been getting as much sleep," I replied, with a light yawn.

As Asia leaned against the manufactured wall that enclosed my cubicle, I noticed her new diamond tennis bracelet. It sparkled gently and looked like it cost a pretty good amount.

"Dang Asia boo. I see you blinged out. When you get that?" I asked.

"Oh I meant to tell you about this," she said, smiling. She pulled her arm away from the cubicle and started to examine the bracelet, turning it on her arm.

"Drew got it for me. He was offered a job Monday that pays really well. We all went out to dinner to celebrate and he surprised me with this. I'm not even sure how he paid for it. I didn't ask. Prolly charged it on his credit card. We went through a really rough patch these past couple of months and he said he appreciated me for being there for him and never judging."

"Well it's beautiful," I admitted. "Guard it with ya life, or else I might steal it," I joked, laughing.

"Aight girl, well I was just checking on you. I'ma call you later and we can play catch up. Plus you never told me if you apologized or not. I'm gone tho, I'ma call you." She walked off and left me with some unanswered questions.

Asia hadn't been acting strange or anything but it seemed like she may be hiding something. Her bracelet looked like it had cost at least a grand, so why hadn't she told me about it. Most women would have jumped at the chance to brag to their friends about the new diamond bracelet their husband had bought for them. And that was a pretty hefty price for Drew to pay for a bracelet, even if it did go on his credit card. I didn't know if Asia was being 100% honest, but I did know that I would definitely keep my eyes open for wolves dressed in sheep's clothing.

SEVEN

I WAS NORMALLY up by 5am so I could have more than enough time to drop Layla off and be on time to work in Blue Bell by 7am. This morning was different. The sound of my ringing phone woke me abruptly out of my sleep. By the time I clumsily reached for the phone, the ringing had stopped. It was 4am. I had just laid down at 3:15 and I was dog tired. My burning eyes struggled to stay open as I slowly sat up in the bed to check my phone. I had several missed calls from a private number, another missed call from Onney, who had called me around 1am. I wasn't sure how I had managed to miss her call since I was still up at that time.

Just as I was erasing my call log, my phone began to ring again. I answered the call on the second ring.

"Hello?" I asked tiredly, into the phone.

"Hi, is this Nina Washington?" a stern, Caucasian sounding voice asked.

"Yes this is. Who is this?" I asked, a bit puzzled and confused. I wondered why someone who sounded like a telemarketer would be calling at this time of night.

"Ms. Washington, my name is Detective Carl Leonard. It's about your sister Onye Washington."

"Yes. What's going on officer?" I was now fully awake and was growing scared and confused.

"Well you were listed as next of kin for Onye Washington. I'm sorry to tell you this, but we found her several hours ago. -- She's dead. -- Apparently from suicide."

My body grew numb and I suddenly lost my breath. I couldn't scream, I couldn't cry. I was mute. I felt like my life was crumbling around me and I was trapped. I dropped the phone and curled into a ball. Five minutes later, reality sunk in and I was crying like a baby. *Why was everything happening? What did we do that was so wrong?*

At the time I couldn't answer those questions, but I did know that I needed to figure what was going on in my life and get a grip on things. I didn't know if things could get any worse. In all actuality things were just beginning.

I don't remember the four hour drive to Onney's home. Neither Briana nor I were emotionally stable enough to drive, so Eric offered to take us. Even though we weren't super close to Onney, we were still sisters. I had become closer to her more recently with all that had been going on. Aunt Sheena wasn't able to go since she had to work and any deviance from her routine could be a violation so she didn't risk it. She told us to keep her updated with texts and she would call.

When we pulled up to Onney's home the scene was surreal. The house had crime scene tape around it, and there were police everywhere. As I tried to enter the home, I was stopped by several uniformed officers who were guarding the area. I asked to speak with Detective Leonard, who came out in several minutes to usher me and Briana in. As we followed the detective, I peered around the inside of Onney's home and realized she hadn't been very honest with me about her financial situation. Her home was quite lavish for a Lieutenant's salary at a correctional facility. I wondered how she had been holding on this long.

We walked into an empty bedroom where Detective Leonard closed the door and finally begin to speak.

"I'm sorry we had to meet under these circumstances, but I'm Detective Leonard. You're Nina?" he asked, extending his hand to me. He then looked over to Briana.

"And you miss lady, I'm sorry I didn't get your name."

"Oh hi. I'm Briana Washington. Onye's

youngest sister," she replied, in a low weary tone.

"Well ladies, it appears to have been a suicide. She used a gun that was registered to her husband. He was at work when it happened. He works the 11p-11a shift over at the prison. A neighbor heard the gunshot and called it in. Your sister was going through some issues with depression. She has a prescription made out to her in her purse. Her husband didn't even know about it.

I wasn't surprised by what he was saying. It actually all started to make sense. She had said she was going through other things, and it was a lot on her.

"The main reason I brought you in here today however, was because although your sister was going through depression she was also under investigation at work. She was suspended yesterday pending the outcome of investigation." He studied our faces closely to watch for a reaction.

"Oh my god," we both gasped. "For what?"

"Well, apparently she had been accessing

private inmate information and using it inappropriately. The investigation is still ongoing, but from what I was told, there was a possibility that criminal charges would be filed."

I felt as if I had been hit in the gut with a sledgehammer. Onney had taken her life because someone had found out she had been accessing prisoner information. There's no telling what else they knew. The feeling of guilt flowed through my body, so I placed my hands over my face and shook my head while I cried silent tears. Briana stood there stunned as well. As much as I wanted to cry out in true sorrow, I couldn't: it would look too suspicious.

"Ladies I am sorry for your loss. If there's anything I can do to help you, or if you have any questions, please call me. I'll give you two a moment alone to gather yourself. I'm sure you're ready to begin making arrangements for her."

He handed me his business card while I lifted my head up long enough to thank him and take the card.

I looked at Briana and said nothing. The look I gave her confirmed that we had a whole lot to discuss. However, Onney's house was definitely not the place to do it. Lord knows who was listening.

Before we left, I went to speak to Onney's husband Kevin, who was sitting in the kitchen answering more questions from detectives. After they finished speaking, I gave him a hug and explained to him that although I didn't know him, I was there if he needed me. He gave me his number so I could help him make arrangements for Onney. I could tell he had been drinking but I said nothing.

The week that followed was very emotional and hectic. We laid Onney to rest in a small, quiet ceremony in the town she lived in. The turnout was small since she didn't have much family, however, a few loyal friends from her job showed up to pay their respects. According to her husband, many of her fellow officers did not show up because of the scandal of the investigation. Of course Onney's husband walked around intoxicated most of the day, but he was still respectful and helped me lay my sister down to rest properly.

When I laid down to bed the night of the funeral, I prayed to Onney, and I prayed to God, asking them both for forgiveness. I felt nothing but sadness and guilt behind getting Onney involved with this scam of mine. There was no way that I would file another single tax return that was illegal. I had made most of the money for the blackmail to end, and whatever I didn't have I would take it out of my account. All I could pray for was that whoever was doing this would let me move forward, and that the IRS didn't catch up with my black ass.

A month had passed since Onney's suicide, and I still struggled daily with grief and feelings of guilt. Briana and I were at odds once again. Lately she had been acting odd and very distant. I would call her and she would call me back days later. I would stop by her home, and she would not answer the door. When I did manage to catch her she would run back and forth to the bathroom in fifteen minute increments. If I didn't know any better she was either pregnant, or god forbid, on drugs.

I turned left off of Broad Street to the parking lot of McDonald's, at Broad and Allegheny. I was there to pick up my Aunt Sheena from work, so we could go have an early dinner before her curfew at the half-way house she was staying at. She was due to be released from there in a week, and I wanted to talk to her about her next move.

I looked down at my watch and it was 6:02. I knew Aunt Sheena would be walking out any second. She didn't like working at McDonald's and when it was time for her to leave she didn't play any games. Right on cue, she walked out the door, smoothing her ponytail out after taking off her work hat.

"Dang Aunt Sheena, you didn't even bother to change." I laughed, before giving her a kiss on the cheek.

"Girl, I aint got time for that shit. I was ready to go. Them motherfuckers was getting on my damn nerves today too," she huffed.

"Where we headed?" she asked, still trying

to fix her hair.

"Well, I was just going to go Downtown so we could eat. I wanted to talk to you about something anyway.

"Aight cool. I don't want to be too far from the half-way house anyway, since I gotta be in by nine." She looked down at her stained uniform. "I'll change this shit in the bathroom. I got my clothes in my bag."

Aunt Sheena sure could be ghetto as hell, but I loved every bit of her. She always kept it real and never sugar coated shit.

Where's Layla?" she asked, after looking in the empty back seat.

"She's with her dad. Ever since Onney passed he has been staying some nights at my house to help me out. He's off on the weekends so it helps me get a lot done."

Aunt Sheena looked at me with a smirk on her face. "Ummm hmmm...I see somebody back over there knockin them boots out."

If I was light-skinned my face would have turned blood red. My aunt sure knew she would say any damn thing. Over the past month we all had grown really comfortable together, and Aunt Sheena was proving to be just as outspoken as she wanted to be.

"Naa. It's not like that. He really is helping me out," I smiled.

Aunt Sheena and I got a small booth in a quiet section in the back of Applebee's. We both ordered the parmesan sirloin, and drank Strawberry lemonade while we waited for our food to come.

"So what did you want to talk to me about? Aunt Sheena asked, initiating small talk.

"Well I don't know how to put this." I paused. "I know it's kind of a sensitive subject for you-- But recently I've noticed Briana's been acting weird." Aunt Sheena raised her eyebrows in curiosity. I continued.

Maybe you've noticed it too. She barely answers the phone and returns calls. When I am able to get up with her she acts really weird, running back and forth to the bathroom. And most recently she hasn't been keeping up on her appearance. She looks like shit and her hair was a wreck last time I saw her. I think something's going on with her. Maybe she's pregnant, depressed, or worse, on drugs." I waited for her to respond.

Aunt Sheena shook her head in dismay. "I fuckin knew it. I saw it over a month ago when she came to pick me up from work one day. She seemed spaced out. I peeped the signs but I dismissed them because it was Briana and I didn't want to believe it. If she is on drugs, it's because of the nigga Eric. I had been meaning to tell you who he was." She paused before continuing.

"You probably never heard about it, but about six years ago, before I went to prison, there was some jack boys running around Philadelphia robbing stash houses. Well, Eric had a couple of them in West Philly. One night one of his houses got ambushed and his cousin was murdered. According to the streets, Eric killed about four people who were involved with his cousin's death, including a pregnant female. He ended up getting locked up but beat the charges. The witness never showed up to testify. From the stories I've heard, the nigga was a menace. I personally didn't know him but he was very well known through the city. His case was on the news." She shook her head.

I stared at Aunt Sheena in disbelief. "How come you didn't tell me this? I'm sure Briana has no idea."

"Nina baby, I just found out it was him, and honestly I didn't know how to tell you. One thing you gotta understand about Briana is she's going to do what she wants. That boy got her gone over him. She out here trying to be hood, doing the shit he doing. She's in love with him and he can't do no wrong in her eyes. That's something that you're not going to be able to come in between. You see how fast she knocked you upside ya head over something you said about the nigga. Imagine trying to get him out the picture. You also gotta remember that she's 26, not 16. You can't tell her what to do." With that being said, I sighed uncomfortably.

Briana is a lot like your mother and I were. She's weak minded and she looks for love in the wrong places. You're not going to be able to compete with the man she thinks she's in love with. The best way to be there for Briana is to never let her get too distant, stay in contact with her, and as hard as it may seem, never speak ill of Eric," she said with a serious face.

I stared at Aunt Sheena for a second and then picked up my glass to take a sip of lemonade to get rid of the lump that had formed in my throat. At the end of the day Aunt Sheena was right. There wasn't much I could do but talk to Briana. I would definitely confront her about her potential drug problem, but I would do it when the time was right. For now, I would pray to God and beg for his mercy for my sister.

During the drive home I realized I had never talked to Aunt Sheena about her living arrangements for the upcoming week. Although I loved my aunt, I wasn't sure about her living with me because of Layla. I instead, had been thinking about offering her some space at one of my properties.

My largest property in North Philly had a basement that I could have converted and livable in a week. I would just get one of my guys to add some carpet. I had actually intended on renting that out as a studio since the plumbing was in order to add a kitchenette. Surprisingly, the previous owner had installed a small, but functional bathroom. I guess they had the same idea of it being a studio. I figured it would be perfect for Aunt Sheena if she wanted it.

I took a detour from my home and decided to go by Briana's to check on her. It was a little after nine so I knew she would be up. Before I got out of my car I called her phone, but of course there was no answer. Seeing her car, I got out and went and knocked on the door. Not surprisingly, a nigga answered.

I recognized the brown-skinned guy from the casino the night Briana met Eric. He smiled flirtatiously when he opened the door.

"How you doin baby," he asked. I could smell weed permeating off of his clothes. I held my breath to keep from visibly cringing.

"I'm fine. My sister home?" I asked, barely letting myself in the house through the small space he had made at the doorway.

"Yeah she here," Eric said, standing up, when I walked in the door. I'll go get her for you.

"No that's okay, I wanna go back and show her something. That's cool right?" I said, not really asking. I was trying to hurry up and get to the back of the room with Briana. The sight of Eric made my skin crawl.

"Yeah that's cool," he responded, insincerely.

I made my way to Briana's bedroom. To my surprise, she wasn't there. When I turned around to walk out, I noticed Eric had followed me in the room. He closed the door behind him and locked it.

"Where's Briana, I thought you told me she was in here." I asked, growing instantly afraid. The sight of Eric and knowing he was a possible murderer was really giving me the heebie jeebies. I was growing fearful.

"Why would you lock the door? I damn

sure didn't come here to chill if Briana's not here."

"I just wanted to talk to you about something." He smiled, while running his hand over his head of neat cornrows.

"Ok. Well talk. And you can open the door to do that," I said, glancing over to the doorway.

Ignoring my request, he began to speak. "So I heard from Briana that you don't like me."

"I never said I didn't like you," I answered, keeping the conversation to a minimum. After all he was an alleged killer.

"For some reason, I don't believe you," he responded, with another smirk.

"It's a shame too, because you would really enjoy my company if you got to know me." He then did the unexpected and grabbed his crotch area in a crude manner.

Before I responded I inconspicuously reached in my purse and felt to see if I had my mace. This nigga was on some other shit.

"Let me get something straight with you. You're right. I don't care very much for you. A lot of you nigga's is users and leeches. My sister has a little more than the average bitch and nigga's try to take advantage of that. It's also nasty ass gestures, like the one you just made, that makes me not fuck with nigga's like you. Now I don't want no beef with you, but I'd appreciate if you open the door and let me the fuck out."

Somewhere inside of me I had the courage to just say what I said. In all actuality the nigga had me shook. I made eye contact with him while I waited for his response.

Eric smirked and then unlocked and opened the door. He still didn't move, so I brushed past him on my way out. The whole time he indiscreetly stared me up and down shaking his head in satisfaction. I regretted wearing the curve hugging dress I had just bought from The Pink Elephant.

I made my way out of Briana's house while Eric's two friends made kissing sounds and cat-calls. I called Briana's phone as soon as I got in my car; of course she didn't answer. I told her to call me but left the part out about Eric talking slick to me at her house. She wouldn't believe me anyway, and even if she did, she would probably take his side before mine. I chalked it up and decided with her, some things are better left unsaid when it pertained to Eric.

◇◇◇

When I got home Layla was sleep and Rashid was in the living room watching television. He'd been there since Onney had passed, and actually, he made me feel much safer. I plopped down beside him after saying hi, and kicked off my heels. I had a long day.

"I see you found my liquor stash," I laughed, after noticing the small glass he had that appeared to be filled with vodka and orange juice.

"Yeah, Layla wore me out. It's some pizza in the kitchen if you want some," he offered. I smelled the alcohol on his breath and quickly realized he hadn't just started drinking.

"Na, I ate out with Aunt Sheena." I yawned lightly. "I'ma go take a shower and hop in bed. I'm tired. Don't forget to cut the

T.V off."

"Aight," Rashid responded, looking up at me with glossy eyes. I could tell he was almost drunk. Surprisingly, he never really could handle much liquor. If he was going to do drugs he should probably stick to weed.

I was sleep when I felt someone crawl into my bed. When I felt the hands grab my waist, I realized it wasn't Layla. It was Rashid. My heart instantly began to pound, however, it wasn't from fear; it was from arousal.

"Rashid what are you doing?" I asked, my breathing accelerating. I already knew what he had come for.

"Shhhhhh," he whispered drunkenly into my ear. "Chill. I just want you for tonight. I promise I won't say nothing else to you about us. Just give me tonight." He leaned over me, kissed my chin and proceeded to pull down my panties. I wanted to say no, but I remained silent. My mind was frozen, but my body was melting.

My mouth just would not open to respond. My body spoke for me and Rashid took full advantage. He licked and sucked my nipples until they stood firm and hard against his toned chest. He kissed every part of my body, not missing a spot. What we were doing wasn't right, however, he felt too good to stop, and I was long overdue for what he was about to give me.

Rashid sucked my toes, and then made his way up my legs and thighs with his tongue. He stopped right in my center, which I exposed fully for him to enjoy. Grabbing my thighs to scoot me down, he then sucked and licked at my pussy until it was wet and running like a faucet. I shuddered from delight. Just as I was about to cum, I pushed his head away and he rose up, eagerly stuffing his nine hard inches inside of me.

Rashid fucked me hard and good that night. When the morning came, reality struck for me, and I asked myself what mess had I just created.

EIGHT

It was finally the first week of May, and I had been getting a call almost every day from the blackmailer. Most of the money from the returns had already been direct-deposited into the multiple accounts I owned. Because it was such a large deposit, I was instructed to spread the transactions out over multiple accounts.

I was ready to get the deposits done so I could move on with my life. I called Briana and she agreed to be ready by ten in the morning so we could head to Bank of America bright and early. A week before, I had informed her it was important for her to be reachable since this was such an important matter.

Things had actually started to look up in my life. Rashid and I were getting along well and I was considering a possible reconciliation with him. Aunt Sheena was out of the half-way house, and was living at my studio apartment in North Philly. She was doing very well with work and staying clean. I was very proud of her, and having her in my life was a huge blessing. She filled a void I never knew existed. We also hadn't heard anything about the investigation from Onney's job.

I pulled up to Briana's home at 9:55 am. Since I was a little early, I decided to go in. I knocked on the door and wasn't surprised when it took Briana five minutes to answer it. I didn't say anything, I just gave her a look to hurry up. I noticed Briana had bags under her eyes and looked extremely tired. She raced through her house in sweat pants and a t-shirt, trying to get ready so we could leave.

"Hey Briana," I called to her. "I'ma use the bathroom while you finish getting ready. I gotta pee after drinking all that Iced Coffee this morning."

I quickly used the messy bathroom and flicked my hands dry in the sink. "Briana you got some lotion?" I yelled. She was in her powder room getting ready, so I went into her bedroom to get some lotion since I hadn't brought in my purse.

Briana's room was also a mess. On her dresser was about a dozen bottles of Victoria's Secret lotions, however they were covered by a stack of wrinkled papers. Being nosey I picked them up to read them. Quickly scanning them, I thought I was seeing things. *It can't be*, I thought. *No fucking way*. I wiped my eyes and looked again. Instantly my heart raced, and anger brewed in my body.

I couldn't believe my eyes, but they damn sure weren't lying to me. The papers were from Bank of America, and they were the welcome papers for the three new accounts made out to Briana Washington and Eric Smith. I pulled out my phone to confirm that my mind wasn't playing tricks on me, but the account numbers did indeed match those that had been sent to me by the blackmailer.

The anger I felt was immediately replaced

with hurt when I confirmed what I already knew. The account numbers in my phone matched those on the papers I was holding. Briana was the blackmailer. I couldn't believe that my own sister was extorting me for money. I left out the room feeling sick to my stomach, but not before grabbing the papers. I was going to confront the bitch.

"Briana what the fuck is this?" I asked, storming into the powder room where she was putting on makeup to fix her disheveled appearance. My voice was laced with anger and I had started to tremble from the emotions building up in my body.

"What?" she asked confused, while using her hand to block the stack of papers I had just hurled.

"Bank of America papers Briana?" I asked her. My facial expression was distorted with the look of hurt plastered on it. I stood in the doorway of the powder room and waited for an explanation from her. Thirty seconds passed and that explanation never came. Instead, Briana stood there like a kid being chastised and no explanation of why they did what they did.

"How could you blackmail your own fucking sister? On top of that, you kept doing this shit even after Onney took her own life behind it!" She stared at me scared with tears welling up in her eyes.

"Onney died behind this shit Briana!" I screamed. Words couldn't express the way I felt. Still standing in the doorway my heart beat rapidly, sweat formed on my nose, and my mind was giving me silent instructions to hit Briana.

"I—I don't know Nina. I didn't mean for any of it to happen. Please let me explain. I—I—It's not my fault. I'm fucked up. I overspent and I didn't know how to come to you. Plus Eric said..." she stammered, visibly shaken.

"Eric said what! To stab ya fucking sister in the back! Why Briana? Explain that?!" I asked, my voice cracking.—Still no answer, so I continued my tirade.

"Because you're selfish! Do you have any

idea what this has done to me? Done to Onney! Her husband! Of course you don't! Because all you give a fuck about is ya fucking self and Eric. All you care about is feeding your fucking drug habit!" She looked at me with guilt and anguish laced on her face.

"Oh what you didn't think anyone knew? I asked in disbelief. "You walk around looking like shit. Running back and forth to the bathroom to get high. That nigga got you looking stupid and he's out here living his life, using you for every penny he can get from you. You wouldn't have seen much of that money, because he would've used it up or been gone with it."

"Ni--Ni---Nina, I'm sorry," she cried, walking towards me.

"Bitch don't come near me." I spat, walking backwards out of her reach. We weren't kids anymore and she wasn't just going to do something fucked up and I forgive her like I usually did. This was the ultimate level of deceit. This was different.

"You sent someone to my house...My home where I rest my head with my child to muscle me... You ain't shit Briana, and if you weren't my sister I'd pound on ya ass." I slammed my fist into my other open hand for emphasis.

"I'm so sorry Nina. I swear. Let me explain," she pleaded.

Her pleas however, fell on deaf ears. I didn't want to hear shit the bitch had to say. I had to leave quickly before I did something I would regret.

I shook my head from side to side and responded, "No you're not Briana. You're sorry you got caught. But you reap what you sow sister," I said, with venom dripping from my voice. I looked at her with rage in my eyes and continued.

"Starting now, you're dead to me bitch. Live and die with ya choices."

I shook my head in disgust and turned around to walk out of the room. Briana fell into her chair and sobbed, but I didn't care. The bitch could rot in hell for all I cared.

My sister wasn't crying because she had wronged someone else and felt guilty. Her snake ass was crying because of her own situation. In my mind, Briana was the lowest of the lowest. What kind of person would continue with blackmail when they lost their sister behind it? Right now I had to get away from her before I wound up doing something I regretted. I vowed that I would not allow my life to crumble at the hands of another. I had to do what I had to do for Nina, since others were doing it all for da doe.

I had no idea that this was the beginning of more to come. Had I known what was headed my way, I would have ran fast away from Philadelphia. The drama wasn't over just yet; in fact, it had just begun.

Check out the following Sneak Peeks for my upcoming books *All 4 Da Doe 2* and *Deceit, Lies, and Alibi's*…Available Soon on Amazon and other online book retailers.

Coming Soon: ALL 4 DA DOE 2

Find out what's next for Nina....

After finding out the identity of her blackmailer, Nina has decided to stay on a legal path, and build her rental property business. Although driven and still very ambitious, Nina has quickly begun engaging in dangerous activity due to the stress of her troubled past. Things still aren't easy as she struggles to protect her misguided baby sister Briana, as well as something even far more precious. More secrets are revealed; more lies uncovered and Nina finds herself questioning everyone for her own sake. Will Nina's own hands ultimately cause her fall or will someone else's. As the drama unwinds this time around, will Nina hold or fold?

Sneak Peak of ALL 4 DA DOE 2

I WOKE UP abruptly from the blaring sound of my phone going off. The ring was piercing and had also woken up Naseef, who was slowly stretching after being spooned against me for several hours. I reached over to his nightstand and grabbed my phone just as the ringing stopped. I wiped sleep out of my eyes to see who it was. It was Aunt Sheena. It was 11pm, which was still early to a night owl like myself. However, it was late for Aunt Sheena who was now working the 5am opening shift at McDonalds.

I quickly scanned through my messages

and saw that she texted me. *It's important. Call me ASAP.* I quickly dialed her number to see what was up.

"Hey Aunt Sheena," I asked, as soon as she picked up the phone.

"Nina where are you baby? I need you to meet me at Temple Hospital in the ER." Her voice was shaking.

"What's going on Aunt Sheena?" I asked, becoming worried. I pushed myself up and sat up straight in the bed.

"It's Briana...Someone found her. She overdosed."

My aunt's voice trembled with fear. I lost my breath and felt like I was about to pass out the moment she spoke those words. However, my sick feeling was quickly overcome with panic that forced me to move.

"I'm on my way Aunt Sheen." I hung up the phone and quickly jumped out of the bed to get my clothes on.

"What's the matter?" Naseef asked me. I couldn't respond. My mind was focused on one thing and one thing only: my sister. I grabbed my belongings and hurried out of the house. There was no traffic on City Avenue coming out of Bala Cynwyd so I was able to quickly hop on I76, and take the Broad Street exit to Temple University Hospital.

The drive was like déjà vu all over again. It was the same feeling I felt when I went to Onney's; dread. I prayed this time that my sister would be okay. I don't know what I would do if Briana was dead so I tried to stay positive. I knew one thing; if she was gone I wouldn't be able to live with myself for shutting her out of my life, regardless of what she had done. Something had to change with us, and it had to change quickly.

My heart raced as I threw my car in park in front of the automatic doors that read *EMERGENCY ROOM*. Disregarding the fact that it was a no parking zone, I ran through the doors and was met by my Aunt Sheena who was standing in the lobby talking to a stern faced, middle-age, white man in a lab coat. As I approached the two of them, I saw his badge and realized he was the doctor. Dr. Vick was his name.

I rushed to my Aunt's side as Dr. Vick spoke. Surprisingly, Rashid was already there. He stood up and came by my side as soon as I walked in. I managed to force a worried smile on my face. I appreciated Rashid being right there for me but I couldn't help the feeling of guilt that weighed down on me. After all, I had just left from Naseef's house.

"Is she okay?" I asked, looking to the doctor while choking back the sob that was begging to escape. I looked at the doctor, my eyes pleading for confirmation.

Aunt Sheena looked to the doctor and said, "It's okay, that's her sister." The doctor cleared his throat and went on to explain.

"Right now my team is doing the best they can to keep anymore of the drugs from absorbing into her blood stream. We injected her with Naloxone, which reverses the effects of the Opioid, however, she had a lethal amount of Heroin in her system, her blood pressure had dropped tremendously and she was almost in a coma when she arrived. She will definitely need to be closely monitored for the next few hours to make sure the overdose process has been eliminated by the Naloxone. Luckily someone found her when they did. Our goal now is to keep her alive. If we are able to do that, she will need a lot of support as well as some aggressive drug rehabilitation treatment. Judging by the marks on her body and her health condition, this isn't something that occurred over night. There's been some ongoing drug abuse. The man she was with showed no signs of drug abuse, but he was pronounced dead at the scene." Doctor Vick continued to talk but I heard no sound, all I saw were his lips moving.

After he mentioned that she was with a man, my mind zoned out, I didn't hear anything else he said. I knew it had to be Eric. All I remember was feeling the doctor pat my shoulder gently, and whisper words of encouragement. He then walked off quickly down the long hall. At that moment I became overcome with grief. I felt as if I was going to throw up, so I took a deep breath and forced a dry swallow.

As I buried my face in my hands to sob, I felt Rashid wrap his arms around my body to console me. My cries were muffled against his work-shirt. I shook off the feeling of guilt and focused solely on my grief. I looked over to Aunt Sheena who was now sitting in a waiting chair with her face buried in her hands, weeping.

Tears rolled down my face as I prepared to spend the remainder of the night in Temple Hospital's emergency room. Without bothering to close my eyes, I quietly took my head from Rashid's chest and looked off to say a silent prayer to God. I prayed that he get Briana through this ordeal. She had done some fucked up shit but it wasn't her time. I wondered how she had gotten hooked on Heroin, but then again I was too busy being angry, and drowning my pain with alcohol.

Get your copy of All 4 Da Doe 2 on amazon.com and other online book retailers for 99 cents. !!!

Coming Soon FREE for a limited time: DECEIT, LIES, AND ALIBI'S

Meet Noah...

Handsome and orphaned Noah grew up poor like most kids from North Philly. Refusing to accept poverty as his fate, he along with his childhood friend Hakim, jacked their way to the top. Years later, he's on a legal path and building a future with his beloved fiancée Shaleea. However when slick talking Eve comes into the picture, love triangles form and everything that Noah has is threatened. Friends are foes, everyone is out for self, and loyalty is no more. As love and lust intertwine, tempers flare and life changing mistakes are made. The stakes are high in this hood tale filled with deceit, lies, and alibis.

ENJOYED THIS TITLE? PLEASE LEAVE A REVIEW OR COMMENT. ALSO, CHECK OUT MY OTHER TITLE *DECEIT, LIES, & ALIBI'S*

Sneak Peek of
DECEIT, LIES, AND ALIBI'S

Chapter 1

Present day

Noah saw his former life flash before his eyes as he stood over Eve with his hands wrapped around her throat. He thought of all that he had, and all that his life was before her scheming ass had come into the picture. He cursed the day he had met her. Instead of his surroundings, he saw nothing but red through his pupils. The sounds she made became muffled and distant. Noah's heart beat rapidly and before he realized it, he had completely blacked out. It was too late.

18 months ago
Eve

It was four a.m. and Eve had been on her computer for several hours. This was her work time and she was in grind mode. She was used to staying up till the wee hours of the morning updating her profile on different internet sites. Eve was an escort and earned her money by having sex with men, however, she liked to consider herself an entertainer. She frequently told people she was a dancer, since she wouldn't dare tell them she was an escort or prostitute.

She continued to work on uploading her most recent photos, being careful to select those that highlighted her most popular attributes: her tiny waist and fat ass. Eve wasn't traditionally pretty. She had strong facial features that sometimes made her appear a bit masculine, however, her Haitian heritage gave her somewhat of an exotic look. With some makeup and sexy clothes she certainly managed to make many men's heads turn. After all, she had to attract men; they were here bread and butter, and the only way she knew how to survive.

Eve wasn't dealt the greatest hand in life. One of four children to an illiterate, immigrant single mother, Eve had always been poor. Eve's mother had migrated with her siblings to America when Eve was just the tender age of 15. With a poor economy, no education, and little skill to obtain a job, Eve's mother Rosa struggled to raise her four children. Back in Haiti, she had relied on prostitution to care for them.

When Eve became old enough, she too turned to prostitution to earn money. She thought back to her early teenage years in Haiti when she used to sleep with white men who came to trade goods on their boats. Eve's body had developed very early, and in her adolescent years she had a body many grown women envied. Men and boys alike loved her dark chocolate skin, her full lips, and her thick thighs and ass. The first time she took goods in exchange for her own "goods" she was 12 years old. She remembered the day...

It was hot, and the sun beamed heavily on her small back. She was hungry and her mother had sent her down to the trading pier with a few dollars. She was hoping she could use the money to get a loaf of bread to go with a pot of broth her mother had been trying to prepare. They were desperate, and their food supply was beginning to run out. Rosa was getting older, and because of a poor diet and lack of proper medical care, her looks and health were deteriorating quickly. She could no longer sway the white traders with propositions of sex, so she sent Eve.

When Eve arrived at the boat she knew what she had to do. With a seductive smile and a lustful tone, she told a middle-age, white trader what she wanted. She then explained to him she only had a few dollars, however, she had something else more valuable than money. The trader knew exactly what she spoke of, and frankly he didn't mind a bit. He smiled back at the young Eve, and she knew she had him.

"Follow me," he said. "You take care of me and I'll take care of you."

So she did just that. Many times Eve had listened to her mother and even spied on her and countless men having sex. Although still a virgin, she knew exactly what to say and do, to satisfy a man. When Eve got to the back of the boat she wasted no time straddling the aging white man on the small makeshift sleeping area. She told him to close his eyes and then she kissed him softly on his chest and neck.

She pulled open his shirt and proceeded to rub his shoulders. She didn't want to spend too much time on the boat so she decided to get down to business. She eased down the traders pants and took him deep into her mouth. She ignored the smell of old sweat and focused on making him cum quickly. She bobbed her head up and down swiftly, sucking furiously, while making loud slurping sounds.

"Ummmmmm," she moaned. "You're so big," she said between slurps, hoping to get him off quickly. That too she had learned from watching her

mother.

As soon as she purred the words he came violently, grabbing her hair, his body twitching. He was done, and she praised herself for being skilled enough to get him off so quickly.

When it was all over, Eve had enough to last her and her family several days. Her services to the fisherman became routine, and eventually spread amongst the other traders. Thus a monster had just been created.

When Eve's mother announced she had gotten a family visa to America, Eve was ecstatic. She thought her days of prostitution, hunger, and poverty were all over. However, when they got to America she was in for a rude awakening. The area of Brooklyn they lived in was poverty stricken and crime ridden. What made things worse was that her mother spoke broken English and had no education, so she had difficulty getting a job.

They eventually moved to the projects and lived off the welfare system, receiving food stamps and a small assistance check. Eve became extremely envious when saw the other teenage girls her age who were pretty, and well dressed. She wanted what they had, so she began to scheme for months.

One month when check day came, Eve wasted no time going through her mother's purse to find her EBT card so she could take the $750 that would post on the card at midnight. After taking the money from the ATM, she returned her mother's card and headed out into the night. Although she felt guilty she had taken the money, she wasn't concerned that they would be evicted. Their rent was only $30 a month, and she could have that to her in no time. Besides, her mother received over $1000 a month in food-stamps; she would have no problem selling a few in exchange for cash.

Eve used the money to rent a room in a cheap motel for a week. The following day she also went to the nearest hair salon for some extensions. Her final splurge was a quality camera phone. To her, the money spent was an investment. She would use the camera phone to take sexy pictures of herself and post them to the Internet on some escort websites she was hearing about. Fucking was going to be her hustle in the State's too.

The prostitution game had changed. Long gone were the days of standing on the corner waving down cars, and sucking dick in pissy alleyways. That method was more so for drug addicts. Younger girls were now getting money off "the game" by setting up shop in cleaner, more discreet environments such as motel rooms.

Perverts and dirty old men were no longer the only clients; business men, regular working men, and just about anyone was paying for sex. Several girls she knew were making good money, and Eve wanted a piece of the pie.

The first site she heard about, Backpage.com, would eventually become her favorite. She used it religiously along with Escorts.com. Those two sites were where ninety-five percent of her income came from; that and word of mouth. All she had to do was pay a small advertising fee so she could solicit her services to men looking for sex. It really was a win-win situation for her.

Within weeks Eve had men coming in and out of her room. She made enough to have fun, keep her makeup and hair flawless, and keep the latest threads. She actually made a decent income when you considered what she paid to practically live out of motels.

Eventually Eve went to visit her mother to apologize and pay her money back. Although she had been gone for weeks, her mother never worried or questioned her whereabouts. It wasn't unusual for girls to run off at eleven and twelve in Haiti.

Eve told her mother she had a part-time job at a fast food restaurant. She didn't tell her what she was really doing or how much money she was making because she didn't want her begging for handouts. Deep down Eve resented her mother.

Long ago her mother had been married to a decent Haitian man who was also the father of her first three children. When Eve's mother got pregnant a fourth time, rumors were swirling around the village that the unborn child did not belong to her husband. For years her mother had been known for her promiscuity amongst the people of the small community. Nevertheless, the creamy skin of the half Caucasian baby confirmed the rumors when she gave birth. Soon after, her husband left and never returned.

Eve felt that her mother had her chance in life and blew it. Because of her failures, her children suffered and lived miserably, forced to turn tricks and suck old, white dicks just to eat.

Eve refused to be a miserable, failure like her mother. Problem was, that was all she knew. However, Eve felt that if she had to suck dick to make a living she would focus on sucking the right dick. Sadly, she had grown up so ignorant she never knew that if she pursued a proper education she could have had a future. Even if Eve had known, she probably wouldn't have done it anyway. She instead, kept her mind on three things: men, money, and dick.

She hoped to find someone who was paid and that would eventually take her in and provide for her. She met few men she felt were good candidates. Most of them were too old, too broke, or married. Those that were married usually just wanted fun and wouldn't even think of leaving their wives. She couldn't wait till she finally met "The One." Little did she know that he was on his way, and she would eventually get a whole lot more than what she had bargained for.

◇◇◇

Chapter 2

Noah

"Yo, bull," Noah mouthed into the receiver of his iPhone 5, greeting his child-hood friend Hakim.

"Wassup my nigga," replied Hakim, still focused on whipping his Cadillac Deville in and out of mid-day traffic.

"We still going up-top tonight to celebrate?" Noah asked.

"No doubt, my dude," Hakim responded, holding his phone up with his shoulder since his hands were occupied by the steering wheel.

"Pick me up around 8 and we out. Oh, and grab some of that good shit," he said, referring to the exotic weed they both liked to smoke.

"No doubt. I got you. It's ya day. Everything's on me," Noah replied, with a smile.

"Good looking my nigga. See you then. One."

Hakim ended the call and allowed his phone to drop into the plush leather seats.

The two friends went back to their tasks and began to mentally prepare for the two and a half hour drive from Philadelphia to New York. It was Hakim's birthday and after living in Philly for most of his adolescent years, he decided that their club scene just didn't compare to his home-town New York, so he asked Noah to accompany him there for a party being thrown in honor of his birthday.

Noah pulled his Polo hoodie tight against his body for extra warmth against the brisk air. It was surprisingly cold for April, but that didn't stop him from standing outside of his door, blunt in hand, blowing smoke circles into the air. He couldn't smoke in the house because his fiancé Shaleea wouldn't allow it. He adored Shaleea and was always willing to compromise with her to make life smooth. They'd been together 7 years and he'd taken her through hell and back during that time, but she still stuck by him.

Four months prior he officially declared his love by proposing to her on Christmas Eve with a five carat, princess cut diamond ring. It had set him back $10,000, but he gladly paid it since she was worth every penny. She truly was one in a million.

Shaleea was beautiful to him, with smooth skin that resembled fudge. She had a loving and caring personality, and it didn't hurt that she was educated. What really made his love run deep for her was that she wasn't like all the other girls that came and went in his life; she truly cared for him as a person and never worried about his money, or what she could gain from being with him. Her love for him was pure. She listened when he talked, gave him sound advice, and was affectionate. He wouldn't deny that she was good to him.

"Ouch!" Noah winced in pain. While deep in thought, he had smoked his blunt down so low it burned his hand. Throwing down the "roach" and smashing it up with his Timberland boot, he decided he was done. He opened up the oversized cherry-wood door to return back into his modest town-home. He was finally ready to begin preparation for his night out in New York for Hakim's birthday. He was eager to unwind and let loose in the city. Just like his favorite rapper Drake, YOLO was his motto. *"You only live once."*

No doubt he loved Shaleea and wanted to spend the rest of his life with her, but at the end of the day he was a man. Noah felt like it just wasn't in the nature of man to be faithful. *Bend them over, fuck em, and get em out*, was how he went about dealing with hoes. Every now and then if the head game and sex was right, he would toss a few dollars, but none of them would ever get anything close to what he gave to Shaleea; his heart.

Chapter 3

Shaleea

At 8am the cobblestone streets of Chestnut Hill were congested and already bustling with activity. The neighborhood, which was nestled in the Northwest section of Philadelphia, was home to upper middle class residents and had homes that averaged around $600,000.

Struggling through traffic down the bumpy road, 28 year old Shaleea had just dropped her daughter Heaven off at school and was on her way to get a hot cup of coffee from Dunkin Donuts. That was her energy during the week. She needed a caffeinated boost so she could finish writing a paper on Ethics for her graduate class at Temple University. After finishing her paper she would make her rounds to the four laundromat's she and her fiancé Noah owned; Squeaky Clean; one, two, three, and four.

Four years ago, Shaleea had finally gotten Noah to invest some money into a legitimate business for them to build their future together on. They initially opened one small, run-down, 24-hour laundromat in North Philadelphia with $50,000. Noah was a little hesitant to put the money up at first, not wanting to invest too much. As much money as he had tucked away, he certainly was frugal.

With some convincing, Shaleea was able to instill confidence in Noah and let her show him she was capable of running a business. It wasn't that he didn't believe in her; Noah just wasn't into taking monetary losses.

Although the laundromat was run-down, Shaleea saw the potential because of the location. With the help of a few crack-head's and contractors, they had the place looking presentable in no time. To their delight the business did wonderfully. With an aggressive investment strategy in place, they had been able to open a new location every year.

The businesses thrived in the poor neighborhoods of Philadelphia where most families couldn't afford the luxury of having a washer or dryer in their home. Although the laundromat's were in the ghetto, Shaleea focused on making them affordable and comfortable, using her own money she had saved to offer Wi-Fi, air-conditioning, cable television, and free store-bought muffins and fresh coffee. Her goal was to create a professional establishment people wouldn't mind sitting in for several hours while they did their laundry.

Many businesses in urban areas such as North Philly, were ran down and un-kept. She felt poor people deserved decent, clean businesses in their neighborhood just like anyone else. So far, the hard work had paid off and their laundromats were extremely successful, bringing them in a net profit of around $40 thousand per month before expenses.

She hoped to soon convince Noah to open up additional locations in Baltimore. The goal was to capitalize off the urban market by expanding in the inner city. She wanted to be like George and Weezie.

With Shaleea proving her business skills and intelligence, Noah no longer hesitated to hand her his bank card or give her a blank check. In time, she no longer needed his cash to grow; she had her own, along with joint credit cards, and bank accounts.

Shaleea was the brains in the relationship. She had a Bachelor's degree in Finance and was on her way to obtaining an MBA from Temple University. Noah was the muscle and the money, not necessarily earning his small fortune, but taking it through brute force through a small team he and Hakim founded called Torch Boyz.

In the past, Noah didn't discriminate. He started off robbing people as well as small establishments. He eventually moved on to more lucrative capers such as check cashing places, and ultimately bank ATM's. Noah liked to describe himself as peaceful during his dirty deeds. However, in the event that anyone decided to be a tough guy, he would quickly show them he was in charge. He did his best to avoid hurting innocent people, however, that was sometimes inevitable, especially if there was any threat posed against him or his well-being.

Noah and Hakim robbed for many years. As time went on they focused on the quality and not the quantity, targeting ATM's in various cities throughout the country that were known to hold up to a hundred thousand dollars at once. Over time, several ATM's in a night quickly put the pair where they wanted to be financially.

Those days however, were in the past. No longer wild and reckless, Noah was now a businessman who hoped to grow his businesses and expand his portfolio to soon include real estate. He was extremely stable financially and had a decent amount of "old" money he wanted to invest. He was in love with Shaleea and ready to fully settle down and make her his wife. He also longed for a family and hoped he would eventually achieve that with Shaleea and Heaven.

Noah had lost his mother and father to the streets when he was seven years old. His dad Boogie had been a well-known jack boy in the city. He was known to do whatever necessary to take care of his baby boy and baby-mama. He also had a reputation as being merciless and deadly. However, after years of providing for his family by taking from others, he eventually found himself on the opposite end of the gun.

Boogie and his girl Pam, Noah's mother, were brutally gunned down in their home late one cold, December night. Police never made any arrests. However, word on the street was someone killed him out of revenge.

After Noah lost his parents he found himself in and out of foster homes longing for a stable family. He sincerely appreciated Shaleea and Heaven because of the stability they gave him. He felt God gave them to him so he could be whole again; and he did indeed feel whole.

Shaleea had met Noah 7 years back in the Germantown section of Philadelphia. She had just purchased a seafood platter from the Velvet Lounge, and was walking back to her car on Chelten Avenue. Her deep Hershey colored skin, along with her shapely figure is what caught Noah's eye as she walked to her small Honda civic parked up the street.

Shaleea had hips that literally stuck out on her voluputous frame and complemented her heart shaped bottom. Noah was in awe since he'd always been a sucker for a nice body. When he approached her she seemed a bit hesitant to converse with the handsome stranger who stood before her, however his charm eventually put her at ease.

At 6 foot 1, Noah towered over Shaleea's 5 foot 4 curvy stature. He was boy next door handsome with big round eyes that were mysterious and hinted at a dark past. He wore a sharp, low cut Caesar hairstyle, and a full beard around a mouth that revealed a row of shiny white teeth. He had a caramel complexion and a boyish grin that mesmerized and captivated her. She was intrigued by the stranger.

After introducing themselves to one another the two immediately hit it off, standing on the sidewalk talking for almost an hour. They eventually exchanged numbers, with her watching him walk off.

She noticed he was walking as she drove off so she assumed he didn't have a car and used public transportation. In actuality, his car was parked several blocks away and he was simply walking to reach it. Although she didn't know this, she was never bothered by the fact of him using public transportation. She was far from superficial and shallow, having been taught as a child that materials didn't define the man.

Her father was a hardworking man who didn't have a lot of money. However, he had a lot of love in his heart and he was a provider. Shaleea felt that if she could find a good man with a good heart, that's all she would need in this world. Her mother had taught her that behind every good man is a good woman; security and stability would come along with it if they worked together as a team. She didn't mind working and doing her part.

Her mother had worked in nursing as long as Shaleea could remember. She was a strong woman who never received welfare. She stood on her own, and made sure she instilled those values in her four girls. *"No man wants a lazy dumb woman,"* her mother would tell them. *"A beautiful hard working woman is valuable to a man."*

Unfortunately Shaleea's father Tate didn't realize that in the beginning. While he was a good provider, he was a dog who liked to often stray away from home. When Shaleea's mom Gina found out, she left him. She stood on her own since then, never asking him for anything except to take care of his daughters. Luckily for Gina, she was still young and later found a good man named Chris who drove trucks for a living and earned a respectable salary.

To Shaleea, Gina and Chris embodied the American dream of love and success. They weren't rich but they were stable and financially secure; that's the only thing Shaleea wanted.

ABOUT THE AUTHOR

Shontaiye is a bookstore-library freak. She is an avid reader who was blessed with a vivid and active imagination since she was a small child.

She has a Bachelor's in Business and works in emergency services at a large company in Delaware.

When she's not creating fictitious characters, she's going to graduate school for a Master's in Communication. She currently resides by the beach in Maryland, with her daughter and husband. This is her third novel.

Made in the USA
Lexington, KY
17 November 2015